AMANDA BLAKELY & MICHELLE
MCMILLEN

Cry Baby, Don't Cry

MLM
PUBLISHING

First published by MLM Publishing 2025

First edition

ISBN (paperback): 979-8-9929540-1-2
ISBN (hardcover): 979-8-9929540-0-5
ISBN (digital): 979-8-9929540-4-3

This book was professionally typeset on Reedsy.
Find out more at reedsy.com

To my sons, Chase and Hank,
This is my story. I wanted you to hear it from me.

"I struggled for something.
I did something.
I left something."

Contents

1

6053 Pebble Beach

I grew up in a beautiful house on Pebble Beach Avenue in Memphis, TN, though the exact address escapes me now. It remains a dream home in my heart, one that I can still picture:

The house had a two-car garage with two doors: one leading to the backyard and the other into the main part of the house. The kitchen opened up to a spacious backyard that was a centerpiece of our family life. There was a single tree standing in the right corner and a kidney-shaped pool—a playful joke in our family, as we would always laugh about its shape. The pool had a shallow end that started at three feet and sloped down to a depth of ten feet, reflecting my dad's lifelong work as a pool builder.

Inside, the kitchen led to two paths. One way went to the den, which was adorned with rich wooden walls and featured a cozy brick fireplace, fueled by gas. The other door led into a living room filled with eclectic items, including an exercise machine, where my siblings and I would often play school.

Through the den there was another door leading to a hallway. This hallway was a gateway to the front of the house and to the right, a staircase that led upstairs. Straight ahead was a computer room, where we learned to burn CDs and navigate the early days of the internet on dial-up AOL.

To the right of the hallway upstairs, there was a closet where we kept our towels. Straight ahead was my parents' bedroom, which overlooked the backyard through a large window. They had their own bathroom, complete with a shower, while ours had both a shower and a tub.

Exiting their room and heading back down the hallway brought me closer to the front of the house. To the right was my sister's bedroom, and to the left, a spare room. My sister and I would often switch rooms, making playful requests to trade places, a testament to our close bond.

One memory stands out a midst the countless moments we shared: the fire in our house. At the time, we had a babysitter named Nina, who played a significant role in our lives. We affectionately called her "Big Boobie Nina" due to her Double Ds on her small frame. Nina was hired to watch us during the summers while our parents worked—my dad building pools and my mom selling pool products.

While Nina was making us lunch, I found myself in trouble for picking on my sister. Nina instructed me to go to my room and write, "I will not pick on my sister," twenty times. Instead of going to my room, I sneaked into my sister's room to do my "punishment work" at her desk, pretending to be like her while she did her homework.

Suddenly, I heard Nina calling me down the stairs:

"Amanda Nicole Blakely, get down here now!"

I hesitated, reminding her that I was in trouble and had work to finish. But when I finally came down, panic hit me as I saw smoke filling the air. My sister was in the den, and Nina was desperately trying to reach her.

As I rushed down the stairs, I called out, "KiKi! KiKi!" But the smoke was thick, and my heart raced. In the chaos, all my sister knew was to stop, drop, and roll. We called 911, but the fire spread quickly, and the only phone we had was in the kitchen.

That day forever altered our lives, but it also reinforced the bond we shared as siblings and the importance of family in the face of adversity.

The fire started in the kitchen, and we quickly realized we couldn't call 911. Back then, we only had one house phone located in the kitchen, which was intentionally placed there so my mom could overhear our conversations. In that moment of panic, I dropped the phone and ran out the front door, banging desperately on our neighbors' door.

They worked from home, creating custom T-shirts for concerts—everything from Tim McGraw to Faith Hill. When they opened the door, they could see the fear in my eyes.

"My sister!" I exclaimed, just as KiKi rushed behind me, breathless.

"911!" she managed to gasp.

Our neighbors quickly grasped the situation. They called 911 while my sister ran upstairs to use another phone, borrowing it from their daughter, Christy. She was frantic, trying to reach our mom at work. My mom and grandmother worked together at a local business, the Coppertone Company owned by Schering-Plough on Jackson Avenue, and while they couldn't get through to Mom during her lunch break, my sister managed to reach Grandma.

In a flurry of urgency, Grandma got my mom and rushed her out of the break room.

3

"I need to get your purse and your keys. It's not good," she insisted.

My mom, confused and alarmed, asked what was happening, but Grandma held back the full truth to prevent her from panicking.

"I can't tell you right now; just come with me. We need to go now."

I distinctly remember my mom pulling up in the station wagon, with Grandma beside her, both of them running to see if we were okay. That moment of relief and fear is etched in my memory.

After the fire, our lives changed dramatically. We had to rebuild the entire kitchen, and for a while, we relied on takeout for meals—a fun adventure for kids, but I now understand the strain that put on my parents. That experience, while terrifying, became a pivotal moment in our family story, shaping our resilience and bringing us closer together. I'll never forget the lessons learned that day, or the strength we found in each other amidst the chaos.

When I was about 9 or 10 years old, I was my dad's shadow. Being his youngest and a girl, I was his tomboy—his "boy" in every way that mattered. We went hunting, fishing, and four-wheeling together, and I loved it. Whenever his buddies would bring their sons along for these trips, I'd be right there with them, the only girl, but fitting right in.

One particular birthday stands out as a memory I'll never forget. I spent part of the day at my grandmother's house. We did the usual birthday things—talked about swimming, what the plans were, the kind of things you do when you're turning 10. But when my mom came to pick me up, little did I know that my dad had been planning something big.

When we got home, I wandered into the kitchen, feeling kind of bored. I told my dad about my day, probably sounding a bit down.

"It was okay," I said. "But I'm just having a bad day. I wish I could do something fun for my birthday."

My dad, always quick to keep me busy, had an idea. "Hey, babe, can you do me a favor?" he asked.

"I need a screwdriver. Go grab me a Phillips head from the garage."

I didn't think twice about it. After all, I'd always helped him out, handing him tools and fixing things together. But the moment I opened the door to the garage, everything changed. Before I even reached the toolbox, my eyes landed on a brand new Hunter Green Yamaha Big Bear four-wheeler. I froze, unable to believe what I was seeing.

"Oh my God, a four-wheeler! A four-wheeler!" I shouted in disbelief.

My dad walked in behind me, grinning from ear to ear.

"Happy birthday, babe," he said, his voice filled with pride. I could barely contain my excitement.

I think I must have said, "Oh my God" a hundred times in those first few minutes. It was one of the best surprises of my life, and I'll never forget how special that moment was.

Another memory that stands out from that time was how much freedom my mom gave me to express myself, especially when it came to my bedroom. As a kid, my room was pretty basic—just the essentials like a bed and a TV. But as I got older, around 8 or 9, I started getting really into designing my own space. I'd flip through magazines and dream about the kinds of rooms they showed. Claire's, Limited Too, Wet Seal—those stores were everything at the time, and they had the coolest

5

bedroom ideas.

I went through a phase where I was obsessed with canopy beds, the kind with the flowing sheets hanging around them like something out of a fairy tale. I begged my mom to help me turn my room into one of those dreamy spaces, and she was always more than willing. We spent hours together transforming it, painting walls, adding decor, and making it feel like a little slice of life from the magazines I loved.

As I got a bit older, my tastes changed, and once again, my mom was there to make sure my room reflected that.

One day, she said, "Amanda, You're growing up. What are your favorite colors now?"

Without missing a beat, I told her, "Pink and green."

She smiled and said, "Okay, I'm going to do your bedroom for you. If I don't like it, we can always change it, but let's try something a little more grown-up."

I was so excited to see what she had in mind. She had the room painted a beautiful forest green—not too dark, not too light, just the perfect, calming shade. She paired it with white trim, and to my surprise, added touches of pink and yellow. The bed had yellow sheets, and everything else, from the lamps to the accents, was pink. It was the perfect blend of colors, and I loved how mature it felt. It made me realize that my mom wasn't just decorating a room—she was recognizing that I was growing up and helping me express that through my space.

My mom always had an eye for decorating, and I wish I could be as creative as she was. She had this amazing ability to make every moment, every holiday, every room feel special. I think that's one of the biggest things I've carried with me as a mother. I always try to create those kinds of memories for my kids— whether it's making their bedrooms reflect their personalities or going out of my way to brighten their day when they're feeling down. My mom instilled that in me, and I'm so grateful for it. Growing up on Pebble Beach Avenue, she always made sure that no matter what was going on, home was a place of love, creativity, and comfort.

Growing up, I couldn't resist sneaking into my sister's room. You know how it is—every younger sibling wants to peek into their older sibling's world. My sister had a purple room with a futon, and I always thought it was the coolest space. She was a huge fan of *Friends* and had all the DVDs lined up, so whenever I had the chance, I would sneak in and watch them. But the thing I remember most about her room was her Elvis phone. It played "Jailhouse Rock," and whenever it rang, Elvis's hand would spin in a circle. I thought it was the coolest phone ever.

Another vivid memory I have is her playing this game called Tokens. I never really figured out how to play, but I'd always steal the tokens and try to figure it out on my own. By the time she wanted to play, half the tokens would be missing! Mancala was another game she introduced me to, and that became a big part of my childhood. We also spent a lot of time together in the swimming pool. Even though there was a six-year age gap between us, she always made time for me. I felt like her real-life baby, which is why I think she played such a motherly role in my life.

One Christmas stands out in particular. My sister got me the best gifts—a blow-up plastic blue chair, some Hello Kitty lip gloss and watch. It may not seem like much to some, but to me, it was everything. I'll never forget that Christmas because it was just so perfect. My mom also added to those special moments, gifting me a Tinkerbell watch one year. Disney items like that always meant a lot to me.

7

I had a big thing for collectibles. Disney collectibles, in particular—snow globes, figurines, anything that had that special magic to it. It wasn't just Disney, though. My grandmother, my dad's mom, had a love for collecting too, but she was all about dolls. Not just any dolls, but special ones—Shirley Temple dolls, Queen Elizabeth dolls, even Princess Diana dolls. As I got older, we started collecting them together, and that became our thing. When she passed away, she left me those dolls, and they're still some of my most treasured possessions. Collecting those dolls with her is a memory I hold dear, something that keeps her spirit with me even now.

Growing up, we spent a lot of time at my grandmother's house, especially since my dad worked almost every day. He worked Monday through Saturday, with only Sunday as his regular day off. Occasionally, he would have a Saturday off, but that was rare, so my sister and I, along with my mom, often found ourselves at my grandmother's place. It was always full of life, always something happening, because there were so many kids around.

My mom's sister, Melissa, had three children: Karen, Veronica, and Rosalee. Rosalee was from Melissa's second marriage to a Mexican man, who was undocumented, and that's how our otherwise strictly Italian family became more diverse. My mom's side is a mix of Italian and white, but once Aunt Melissa married into a Mexican family, the blending of cultures made our family even more unique.

My grandmother, Judy Carmella Montesi Tiller, was the heart of it all. Her house was a one-story place with a pool in the backyard. That pool was the center of so many memories—it was 10 or 11 feet deep, perfect for diving and playing around. But what stood out even more was the garden that surrounded the pool. My grandmother didn't grow vegetables; she was all about flowers. Her flower garden was beautiful, colorful, and it framed the pool like a work of art. It made the whole backyard feel like an oasis, and it was where all the neighborhood kids would hang out.

We had so many fun times at her house—swimming, playing, just being kids. there were always some complexities with family life too, especially when it came to my Aunt Melissa. She was a nurse, and she would often drive all the way to Nashville to visit people's homes and draw blood for work. But Melissa also struggled with addiction. She wasn't into pills or marijuana, and she didn't even smoke cigarettes, but she had a weakness for crack.

It was like night and day with her. When Melissa was doing well, she was an amazing aunt. She'd take us to the park, we'd ride our bikes together, and she'd set up picnics for us— those were the good times. But when the addiction took hold, things got bad. I can still remember the contrast between those two sides of her—the fun, loving aunt who made everything special, and the version of her that was caught in the darkness of addiction. Despite all of that, there was always love there, and I hold onto the good memories of her whenever I think about those times.

My grandmother's house on Colonial Rd. was more than just a home; it was the center of our world growing up. It was where my cousins and I spent most of our time, and it was the place that held so many of our family's memories. It's hard to describe that house without thinking about all the people who made it feel alive. Me, Karen, Veronica, Rosalee, my sister, and my cousin Marissa—though Marissa wasn't around as much. Marissa's dad, Chris, who was my mom's brother, had his own struggles with pills, so Marissa's mom and her mom's sister ended up taking care of her. They provided everything for her, from private schooling to a stable home, while Chris continued down his path with drugs.

Our family was complicated. Aunt Melissa was a crack addict, while Chris stuck to pills. My grandmother, on the other hand, never touched drugs in her life. She was a strong woman who managed to hold our family together. My mom has always enjoyed her cocktails, but I don't hold that against her, I thank God that she never leaned on any other vices like everyone else in my family—she did the best she could. And, hell, if I were her, I would probably need a drink, too.

That house itself had a certain warmth to it, even during winter when it was cold outside. I'd walk into this big, open space, with a huge window where we used to watch the snow fall. She had a PC—what we called a personal computer—and that's where we learned everything about computers. My grandmother had worked with computers back in the day, so she made sure we knew how to use them, too.

The house was a maze of rooms that connected in a circle. Straight ahead was the kitchen, and to the right, two steps led down to a basement area where she had a deep freezer, an extra refrigerator, and the washer and dryer. The hallway led to three bedrooms and one full bathroom. My grandmother's room was connected to the hallway, and there was a door from her room that led right into the backyard, where the pool was.

One of the most interesting parts of the house was the old wood-burning stove in the den. Long before she could afford a modern oven, my grandmother cooked on that stove, placing firewood into the lower compartment to heat up the top. Even when we got a newer oven, that stove stayed there and became our main source of heat during the winter. It gave the whole house this cozy feeling that I'll never forget.

At our house on Pebble Beach, I have fond memories of our German Shepherd, Smokey Bear. He's the first pet I truly remember. Although there may have been other dogs, Smokey Bear stands out the most. After Smokey, the next dog I recall having was named Blake, which was a white Maltese. Those are the two pets that left the strongest mark on my childhood.

I was born in Memphis, Tennessee, on May 9, 1992, at Regional One Hospital. A fun and somewhat chaotic fact about my birth: my mom was taking my dad's father to a doctor's appointment when her water broke. They had to rush to Regional One, where I was delivered. However, the doctor hadn't arrived in time, so when my head started to crown, the nurse pushed it back, waiting for the doctor to get there. My family believes that this moment might have contributed to my later challenges with ADHD, dyslexia, and other learning disabilities.

One of the most touching stories from my birth is how my dad marked my arrival. He called a radio station to share the news, saying, "Hey, I just had a baby!" The station congratulated him and asked if he wanted a song played. He requested Stevie Wonder's "Isn't She Lovely" as a dedication to me. That song has always held special meaning because of this. Years later, when my oldest son was born, I carried on that tradition in my own way.

When I was growing up, my mom was always there and tried her best to be a good mom. I wouldn't say she was a bad mom, but our relationship was more transactional than anything. She provided for us and made sure we had what we needed—whether it was signing me up for soccer, dance, or helping me with schoolwork—but it was never really about emotional support or unconditional love. When I was feeling down, she would try to fix it by taking me shopping or getting me something to make me feel better. She didn't really provide a space for talking things out or offering a comforting shoulder. Instead, it was always about finding a quick fix.

For example, when I was harassed by a teacher at school, my mom went to battle with the Board of Education to make sure I was heard. She fought for my rights, but even then, it was more about the outcome—solving the problem—than acknowledging my emotions. I can't recall a time when she truly showed pride or unconditional support for me without it being tied to an accomplishment or something I could do for her in return.

In contrast, my dad and I had a closer bond. He wasn't around all the time because he worked so much, but when he was, he was fully present. He taught me how to ride horses, go hunting, fish, and even skin a dove. Those were the moments I cherished with him. He would comfort me when I was having a bad day, and I always felt like I could count on him. Things changed when my son's father, Cedric, entered the picture. My rebellious behavior, the stealing, the totaled cars, and the relationship with someone who they didn't approve of—especially because of racial tensions— damaged my relationship with my parents beyond repair. They couldn't look at me the same way again, and no matter how much I apologized, I couldn't undo the hurt I caused. What I did—stealing, pawned jewelry, money, even guns—wasn't just about the material things; it was about breaking their trust. The principle of it was what hurt them most, and that's something I can never take back.

My sister, on the other hand, has always been there for me. We're six years apart, so our relationship was typical in that she'd get annoyed with me growing up, but I always knew I could turn to her. She's more like a second mom to me, someone I can confide in, but at the same time, it's hard because I know that once the conversation is over, she may not be as understanding as she lets on. She's there for me when I need help—whether it's getting me out of jail, helping with a bill, or just lending a hand. But at times, I know it's wearing on her. She doesn't always want to be the one giving; she also needs support. I've always turned to her instead of my mom because I know she'll help me without judgment or conditions. But even that comes with a price, and I can feel it.

My relationship with my mom has never been the same since I became an adult. It's always been transactional, and there's a wall there that was never truly broken down. My dad, though, after everything that happened, will never see me the same way again either. My sister has the unconditional love that I've always longed for, but I know she's growing tired of it too.

I remember when my sister was going to Ridgeway high school she was throwing a party and when she threw the party everybody was invited: dance team, football players, soccer players, volleyball players, cheerleaders. I mean everybody was coming out. My sister was trying to get rid of me and drop me off at my grandmothers because she didn't want me to go.

I found out about it and I told her, "If you didn't take me then I'm telling mom and dad so you either gotta take me or you're fucked."

Mom and dad were out of town in Rhode Island at some type of ceremony award for the pool company where my dad worked. The across the street neighbor was a retired cop and he saw all

13

of these cars he called to make a noise complaint because he didn't want to be the snitching neighbor. When the cops were called, there were so many people in one house that there was no place for them to run. They all scattered like roaches; people were jumping in the pool, going in the front yard, backyard, and out the windows. There were so many people that couldn't get out in time, they were hiding in our house while the police searched it. Well, of course, as the little sister, I was hiding and went to my room first but there were two people that were already passed out drunk on the bed. Jeffrey, Lorenzo and me went and hid in my sister's room in the closet. The cops came in to ask if anybody was in there and he just told me to be quiet and put his hand over my mouth. He gave it about 10 minutes and when we were coming out,t we looked to see who all was there. Everything was gone: my dad's jewelry, our mom's jewelry, everything had been stolen! The back fence was broken off so there was no back fence anymore. By the time my parents came home, they were just so distraught and pissed off, but we eventually got over it as a family

Mikki, my mom's best friend, has always been a pillar in my life, offering me the kind of love and care I didn't always get from my mom. She treated me like an adult, not in a way that pushed me to grow up too fast, but in a way that made me feel respected. Whether it was taking me to get my nails done, buying me my first name-brand purse, or just spending time with me, she always made me feel valued. Unlike my mom, who would tell me I didn't need things like that, Mikki would make those moments feel special.

When I got older, about 15 to 17, Mikki would take me to her cabin in Pickwick on the weekends. We'd help her fix it up, paint, and do all sorts of work, but we'd also spend hours on the lake, packing sandwiches and just enjoying the time together. It was such a different experience from the way my other aunts were. Mikki was the one who wasn't caught up in the chaos of addiction. She was the one who was always present, steady, and truly good to me.

I could talk to her about anything—things I couldn't talk about with my mom. Even now, I call her for advice, whether it's life advice, financial guidance, or just to vent. She's always been my voice of reason, the calm presence that helped me make sense of things. She never judged me for being myself, and if I made decisions that didn't work out, she'd guide me gently, showing me the way without making me feel bad. Mikki is that peace of mind I never realized I needed, and she's always been there for me.

If I'm being honest, I've always wished I could be her daughter. She was such a good mom to her son, Taylor, even though he struggled deeply with addiction. He treated her terribly—stealing from her and causing her so much pain. But despite everything, Mikki's love never wavered. She deserved so much more than what her own son gave her, and I've always wished I could have been the child who loved her the way she deserved. She's one of the best people I've ever known, and I'll always be grateful for the role she's played in my life.

When it came to my own relationships, I definitely carried those lessons with me. I always knew I wanted a partnership built on trust, mutual respect, and support. But life isn't always as easy as it looks from the outside, and things don't always go according to plan.

As I got older, I found myself facing my own challenges, particularly with my first serious relationship. It was different from what I had grown up seeing, and for a while, I thought I could make it work despite the warning signs. But as things went on, the cracks started to show, and the relationship began to take a toll on me—emotionally and mentally. I felt like I was losing the person I thought I loved, and I didn't know how to fix it.

During this time, I had moments of reflection where I thought about my parents' relationship and the strong foundation they had built. I realized that the kind of love they had wasn't just about being together—it was about being there for each other in every way, even when things got tough. I came to understand that relationships take work, and sometimes, no matter how much I try, things still don't always work out the way I hope.

Looking back, I've learned a lot about myself and what I need in a relationship. I've made mistakes, and there are things I wish I could take back, but each experience has shaped who I am today. Relationships, family, and love are complicated, and even when they're difficult, they teach us valuable lessons.

As I continue to move forward, I try to apply those lessons in my own life. I want to build something meaningful, and I know it won't always be easy, but if I've learned anything, it's that the right kind of love is worth fighting for.

2

Graceful Granny

Granny Edra truly shaped so many of my cherished memories. As she got older and could no longer drive, she never let that stop her from being present. Whether it was birthdays, holidays, or just a simple visit, she always made sure to be there for us. I'll never forget how she'd send us cards with $25 for Valentine's Day. As a kid, receiving mail with money in it felt like the best thing ever.

She had a special way of making holidays unforgettable, too. I can picture her at Target, picking out those timeless Barbie dolls—those iconic ones like the 2024 Christmas Barbie. One Christmas, she went all out and bought Hallmark Barbie ornaments for all of us, and my mom turned it into a theme for our tree. It was a special tradition I hold dear.

As I got older, I had my rebellious moments, and there's that one memory of smoking cigarettes with Granny Edra at thirteen. I know it wasn't the best choice, but it's one of those memories that, in its own way, has stuck with me. On the other hand, she was also the one who showed me the importance of taking care of myself. Granny Edra always looked polished—

her hair and nails done, always well-groomed. I think that's where I inherited my love for beauty treatments and self-care.

I loved spending time with her, especially when she'd let me do her nails or toenails. Those quiet moments, just the two of us, are some of my fondest memories. And the music—country music was her soundtrack. Dolly Parton, Reba McEntire, George Strait, and Johnny Cash always filled her home. That love for country music, that deep appreciation for the classics, is something I carry with me today.

Even though I never knew my grandfather, Granny Edra was a constant, strong presence. She became the dependable figure I needed, showing me what it meant to be both powerful and graceful. She was one classy woman, and I'll always be grateful for the love and lessons she gave me.

Granny Edra was something else. She had this incredible mix of strength and class that made her stand out in a way no one else did. She could break a rock with her words if she needed to, always speaking her mind. But when it came to her own life, she was the epitome of grace and sophistication. She never shopped anywhere less than the best—Kroger, Costco, and Target were her go-to places, but under no circumstances would she ever step foot into Walmart. When it came to medicine, it was always Walgreens, and she wouldn't consider CVS. She was particular, but that's what I loved about her—she knew exactly who she was and didn't settle for anything less.

One of the things that bonded us was our shared love for collecting things, especially porcelain dolls. We'd collect together, and I was lucky enough to inherit her half of the Shirley Temple doll collection when she passed away. Now, I have the entire collection, and it's a treasured memory of her.

There was a time when life was tough for me, and I had

nowhere to go. Cedric, my child's father, and I were on bad terms, and my parents weren't letting me stay with them. But Granny Edra, she never turned me away. My dad, on the other hand, didn't want me anywhere near her house. He had his concerns—he thought I was only after money to be with Cedric, whom he didn't approve of. I overheard him say things about me, but Granny Edra never spoke badly about me to him. She kept those moments to herself.

I remember the routine—I'd show up at her house at night, and she'd let me stay. In the morning, she'd pack me a sack lunch, and I'd leave before my dad came by for his daily coffee and cigarette. This went on for about a month, and it was a bittersweet time. I didn't want to burden her, but she made sure I had a safe space. She never judged me, and I'll never forget that. It was her way of showing love, even when things were difficult.

Christmas at Granny Edra's was always magical. She was the queen of cool gifts, and I looked forward to it every year. She'd get us things like Ugg boots, North Face jackets, and a few outfits, but the best part was always the stockings. They were never just filled with little trinkets—they always had cash. No matter what we got, that extra money would be there, allowing us to get whatever we wanted that we didn't receive. She always made sure Christmas was special for us.

And let's not forget about my parents, who made sure Santa never missed a beat. No matter what, we never went without. That was the beauty of our family—we might have had our struggles, but there was always love, and there was always something to look forward to. And Granny Edra? She was at the heart of it all, making sure we were cared for in every way she could.

Growing up, dogs were always a big part of my life, especially with the pets my grandmothers had. Granny Edra had a brown Pomeranian named Toby, while my mom's mom, Goggy, bred Shih Tzus, and one of them, Angel, was particularly special. Angel was so calm and gentle, never needed a leash, and always came when I called her—she was a real gem, much like Shuga Mama. Granny Edra's Toby, on the other hand, was a little more spunky but still had that sweet, loyal nature.

At home, my dad had a German Shepherd for a long time, and when it passed, we got a pure white Maltese named Blake Snowflake Blakely. These dogs were like family, always there to offer love and companionship. They were my constant companions throughout childhood, and I have so many memories tied to them.

3

1547 Colonial Road

One of the hardest times in my childhood was when my grandmother had five massive heart attacks. I was going to Saint Michael's School at the time, and life changed for all of us. My mom couldn't stay at the hospital with her all day because she had to work, so she made sure someone from the family was always with my grandmother during the day. We, the kids, would take turns. My sister Kiki might go on Monday, Karen on Tuesday, and I would go on Wednesday. We made sure she was never alone during the day until my mom could get off work and take over.

My mom always took care of her mom, handling everything from paying bills to talking with doctors and figuring out home care. My grandmother's other children were often too wrapped up in their own problems. They were going through the house, seeing what they could take, using her car, or even trying to access her bank account, but my mom never lost focus. She became the power of attorney and made sure everything was in order, while her siblings were off battling their own demons.

It was after the heart attacks that my mom made the decision to move my grandmother. She put my grandmother's house up for sale and bought her a new one in Olive Branch, Mississippi. I was around 12 or 13 years old when this happened, and it felt like a new chapter for all of us. A year later, just around Easter time, I remember being in the kitchen of that house in Olive Branch when my mom got the phone call. My parents had finally found a house of their own in Nesbitt, Mississippi. That's when we knew things were changing for the better.

The deep bond with my grandmother shaped much of who I am. Her influence extended beyond language and faith—it was in the way she opened her home, the warmth she shared, and the legacy she passed down. I carry that with me in everything I do.

My grandmother's house was a central hub for our family. It was always filled with love, laughter, and good times, no matter the occasion. Her home wasn't just a place to stay—it was a place where I felt part of something bigger. Whether we were having fun, in trouble, or even doing chores, it was always a great time.

One of the reasons the family felt so grounded was because of our heritage. My grandmother's parents owned a grocery store called Montesi's on Summer Avenue. This was a huge part of our family legacy and played a role in shaping the work ethic and pride my grandmother instilled in us.

At my grandmother's house, even cleaning was a good time. Music would be blasting throughout the house, setting the tone for the day. Everyone had their role: one person on Windex, another waxing, someone else vacuuming. If we finished our chores quickly enough, we'd be rewarded with a trip to the pool or a bike ride to the park. My Aunt Melissa would drive her car alongside us as we biked on the sidewalk, cheering us on as we rode. Sometimes, she'd even join us on her own bike, making it feel like one big adventure.

We also spent hours at the church parking lot next to my grandmother's house, where all the neighborhood kids would gather. Rachel and Sarah, who were sisters, and NeNe and Carly, who were sisters, were part of our crew. Then there were me, Rosalee, Veronica, and Karen, my cousins. My sister and her friend Sharon were older and in their own world, but occasionally they would hang out with us. My sister was closer to Carly, while I ran around with NeNe.

One of the best memories from those days was when it rained for three days straight, leaving a giant mud puddle in the parking lot. The mud was deep, wet, and perfect for making mud pies and giving each other mud facials. We covered ourselves head to toe, laughing and rolling around like it was the best spa day ever. When we finally returned home, caked in mud, my grandmother didn't even get mad.

She just calmly said, "Wash off with the hose, put your clothes in a pile, and everyone needs to take a bath." It was that laid-back, welcoming atmosphere that made her house feel like the heart of our family.

These moments were simple, but they were everything. They taught me the importance of family, laughter, and finding joy in the little things. The memories I have from my grandmother's house will stay with me forever, and they shaped me into the person I am today.

I also remember my Aunt Melissa, who was a larger-than-life character in our family. She was always stylish and loved to stand out. She had two cars—a little blue beater and a white Cadillac. The Cadillac was her pride and joy, and the license plate read "Barbie Girl." That was totally her vibe. With her platinum blonde hair, pink nails, pink lipstick, and blue mascara, Aunt Melissa always made an impression. She had this signature look, and she owned it.

Melissa loved to have fun, and she was the one who taught us how to drive, even when we were way too young. She'd take us to the church parking lot in her little blue car and let us take turns behind the wheel. We weren't actually learning how to drive; it was more about the thrill of pretending. But to us, it felt like the coolest thing ever.

One day, my cousin Karen decided to take Melissa's car on her own—just to drive it around the church parking lot for a bit. It wasn't like she was trying to go anywhere, but Melissa noticed her car was missing. When she realized Karen had it, she marched down to the parking lot, pulled Karen out of the car, and drove it back home. Of course, all of us got in trouble for it. But that was the kind of thing that happened a lot with Aunt Melissa—fun and trouble were always mixed together.

Looking back, those moments felt like small acts of rebellion and freedom. Melissa brought excitement and a sense of adventure to our lives, even when it meant getting into a little bit of trouble.

That memory of NeNe and Amanda Hopper brings up a lot of mixed emotions. It's one of those moments that shows how deeply kids can be affected by the situations they face, and sometimes, the way they respond is their only way of taking back some control.

NeNe was a sweet girl, always taking the high road even though Amanda was relentlessly bullying her. I know the school didn't give her much help because of Amanda's learning disability and her rough home life, but that didn't make it any easier on NeNe. She was constantly picked on, and the situation reached a breaking point when Amanda locked her in the bathroom and tried to beat her up.

When NeNe came to me and told me what happened, I could see the hurt in her. She had been holding back for so long, always being told not to retaliate. But after what Amanda did, it felt like something had to be done. That's when we came up with the idea to invite Amanda over to play on the trampoline. At first, we had some revenge in mind. We thought maybe we could make her feel a fraction of what NeNe had felt by double-jumping her as high as we could on the trampoline, making her lose control for a bit, the way she had made NeNe feel so powerless.

But something changed when we saw her on the trampoline. Maybe it was seeing her in a different environment or realizing that she was just another kid with her own struggles. We didn't end up hurting her or ganging up on her. Instead, we just kept bouncing her higher and higher. It wasn't about violence—it was about letting her experience that uncomfortable feeling of being pushed around, but without causing real harm.

When Amanda finally asked to go home, NeNe spoke up and told her how it felt to be bullied, and that was the moment that stuck with me. Instead of lashing out, NeNe explained her feelings, and Amanda actually listened. She apologized, and even though it didn't fix everything, the bullying stopped after that. It was a strange and powerful resolution, one that I think left an impact on all of us.

Looking back, that situation wasn't just about two kids having a conflict—it was about kids trying to navigate the pain and hurt in their own lives while also learning how to treat each other better. Even in difficult moments, there's always room for understanding and growth.

Another vivid memory from my grandmother's house was the way everything came alive during the holidays, especially Christmas. My grandmother always had the biggest, most beautifully decorated Christmas tree. The whole house would be filled with the smell of baked goods, and she would make these incredible Italian cookies. We all helped decorate the tree, but my grandmother always had the final say on the star—it was her special thing to place it on top. The house was filled with laughter, family, and the warmth of the wood-burning stove. I could feel the love and the tradition in the air, like everything was centered around family and the joy of being together.

We would all gather around in the living room, my cousins, my sister, and I, sitting cross-legged on the floor in front of the fireplace, waiting to open gifts. My grandmother always made sure everyone had something to open, even if it was just a small trinket or a doll. There was never a Christmas where anyone felt left out, and she made sure of that. I'll never forget the smell of pine from the tree, mixed with the scent of the firewood crackling in the stove—it was just perfect.

One year, I got this incredible Tinkerbell watch from my mom that I had been eyeing for what seemed like forever. I was so excited that I wore it every day for months. I also remember the collection of snow globes that started to grow around that time. I had a real thing for Disney, and my family knew it. So each year, they'd add to my collection with a new Disney-themed snow globe. Looking at them would always bring me back to that magical feeling of Christmas at my grandmother's house.

Those were the moments that taught me how important family traditions are, especially during the holidays. Even though everyone wasn't always in the best place in life. Whether it was addiction, stress, or other problems, during the holidays it felt like everything paused. There was peace, joy, and love, and for those moments, nothing else mattered. My grandmother's house was the heart of those traditions, and I think that's why it's such a central part of my memories.

Even as my grandmother aged and went through her health struggles, she kept that spirit alive for as long as she could. After her heart attacks, when we moved her to Olive Branch, things changed a little. The house wasn't quite the same, but the spirit of those family traditions followed us there. Christmas was still a big deal, and I remember my mom really stepping up to make sure that the holidays still felt as special as they always had. My grandmother couldn't do everything she used to, but she was still at the center of it all, watching us, guiding us, and loving us as only she could.

My grandmother's house was at the center of my childhood memories, filled with warmth, laughter, and countless unforgettable moments. One of the most endearing memories was my childhood nickname, "Amanda Boo Boo." I was known for being clumsy and constantly getting hurt, resulting in a new bruise or scrape almost daily. I remember crawling into my grandmother's bed, crying and pleading for everyone to stop calling me by that name.

She comforted me and asked, "What do I want to be called?"

I wasn't sure. She then asked what my favorite animal was, and when I said "cow," she responded, "Well, why don't we call you Amanda Moo Moo?"

I agreed, and from then on, that became my new name. To make me smile, she'd also call me her "little Tinkerbell" because I adored that character. She'd sign my cards with that nickname and lovingly call me Tinker Bell whenever we were together.

My grandmother, whom we all called "Goggy," was also the one who taught every single child in our family how to swim, including helping my oldest son learn. Summers by the pool were filled with music, laughter, and splashes as we cleaned, gardened, or played in the yard. Every moment felt special.

Holidays at Goggy's house were magical and unforgettable. We always spent Christmas Eve there before waking up at my parents' house for Christmas morning. Later that day, we'd visit my dad's mother, Granny Edra. Christmas at Goggy's was special, with the house beautifully decorated and candy canes on the tree for us to pick. Halloween was full of mischief, too. After Goggy went to bed, my aunt would sneak us grand kids out for some fun. We'd roll houses with toilet paper or smash pumpkins—activities that were always a mix of harmless trouble and excitement.

Parties at my grandmother's house were legendary. My aunt would host backyard gatherings with kegs and crowds of 300 to 400 people. The police would show up so often that they knew us by name, usually asking only for the music to be turned down. These parties sometimes lasted for days, with guests cleaning up in the morning, only to start cooking and swimming again by lunchtime, resuming the festivities by nightfall.

Goggy always made sure to be involved in our education, especially mine. She supported me through my learning struggles and advocated for my mom to go the extra mile in helping me succeed. No matter what, she made sure her love and support were felt, whether through schoolwork, holiday traditions, or just the everyday moments spent together.

Playing with other kids didn't happen much in my neighborhood, but at my grandmother's house, it was a different story.

That's where all the memories came alive. We'd meet up at East End Skating Rink and spend hours skating together. The lock-ins were the highlight, and my aunt, Melissa, would always come by around midnight with pizza and snacks to check on us. Sometimes, if I didn't feel like staying the whole night, she'd let me come home with her while the other kids stayed behind. Other times, I'd stay the entire night and have the best time.

I was especially close to NeNe, more than anyone else. Veronica was usually closer to Rachel, but NeNe and I had a special bond. I remember NeNe's mom, Miss Wanda, who always made things fun for us, especially on New Year's Eve. She'd help us make hats with "Happy New Year" written on them and get us poppers and streamers to celebrate. Her kindness and fun spirit made her house a great place to be.

In NeNe's backyard, there was a shed, and between the shed and the fence, Miss Wanda put up a tarp to create a little clubhouse for us. It was like our secret spot with a password to get in. NeNe, in her typical quirky fashion, chose "dirty Band-Aid" as the password. When someone asked for it and didn't know the answer, she'd say no. But when I said, "dirty Band-Aid," she'd let me in with a big smile. Those small moments were the essence of our childhood.

I also remember babysitting my youngest cousin, Rosalee, one day when my aunt Melissa, who often drank white Zin-fandel wine and sometimes did crack, was getting ready to leave. She was likely drunk and had to "run into work" to draw someone's blood and deliver the sample. She got into her little blue car and told me to lock the door behind her. I watched from her bedroom window as she backed out and drove straight into a light pole, bringing it down and totaling the car. Before anyone could react, I rushed outside and brought her back inside to avoid the consequences that could lead to her arrest. The neighbors gathered outside, concerned about the crash, but I stayed silent to protect her.

Another vivid memory was when my cousin Karen got into trouble. Her stepfather, Angel, went outside and chose a switch from a rose bush, one with thorns, and used it to whip her, making her bleed. When my grandmother came home and found out, she was furious.

She confronted him, laying down the law: "You will not lay a hand on Karen or Veronica. That goes for all my grand kids. I can scold them, but I will not hit them. Do you understand?"

Angel, standing in the hallway, apologized and left the house. He went to the store, bought beer, and sat in the driveway drinking, listening to Sublime.

These moments, filled with tension, laughter, and deep bonds, painted the picture of my childhood. Even in chaos or discipline, the love and fierce protection from my grandmother and the closeness with my cousins and friends defined who I was.

I also vividly remember when we would be asleep in the bed with my grandmother. Melissa and Angel would crack the door to see if she was asleep, but I would be awake. I would act like I was asleep, and I would see them go in her top drawer and take her credit cards and they would steal from her. They would run her credit cards up, take her money. They would always say they'd pay her back and never would. Go figure!

They'd always try to make it up to her and do nice things for her, but they never paid her back to the point where it just ran her so fucking dry and left her in debt. My mom stepped in and that's when my mom took it over. My mom had to step in and treat her mom like she was the baby because she couldn't take up for herself. She just couldn't stand up to her kids. My grandmother always tried to give her kids everything that she wanted. My grandmother bought each of her kids, well, each of her daughters their first home. She didn't for Chris, but she did for Melissa and my mom, yet Angle and Melissa always stole from my grandmother and it just wasn't right. Whether it be her medicine, whether it be her credit cards, her bank cards, her checkbooks, they always did that to her. That's when my mom stepped in and had to take over. And I think that's kind of what kept my mom from being able to live her life. My mom always had to live her life for somebody else, so I think my mom never got a chance to live her own life.

I also remember going to Nashville in the summertime. Angel's family lived in Nashville, so we would get dropped off in Nashville and spend the summer with them, and then we would come back and it was the most fun that I ever had as a kid. I absolutely enjoyed every single time of it.

But there was this one time that it just didn't go right. My grandmother, Karen, Veronica and Rosalee were already in Nashville with Melissa and Angel. They went before we did me and my grandmother stayed back and we were going to go together. When we went together, we rode. It was me, Chris and my grandmother and my grandmother was driving the station wagon. I was in the back seat. Chris was in. The front we stopped for gas halfway there when we did, my grandmother went in for gas. My uncle put his hand in between my legs and he tried to stick his finger in my vagina.

I said "No, Stop!" I tried to kick him and kick his hand off of me. He forcefully stuck his finger up there. Now a whole finger did not make it, but it was enough to make blood come out of my vagina.

31

Then he said, "If you say anything, we'll leave you on the side of the road because she'll never believe you. Do you understand? You better not say a word."

So I kept my mouth shut and I waited. I waited all the way until we made it to Nashville. Once we made it there, I went to my Aunt Elda's, which was Angel's sister. That's who we would stay with in her apartment.

I went straight to Aunt Elda and I was crying and she asked me me: "What's wrong, baby? What's wrong? What's wrong?"

I said, "Come with me," and I took her by the hand and I went to the bathroom. She knows English and Spanish very well.

I said "My uncle, he stuck his hand in my private part. and it hurts really bad."

Then, she said, "I don't want to touch you. Baby, go over there. But I need you to lift up your skirt." So when I lifted up my skirt, she said, "Now I need you to pull Your panties down."

When I pull my panties down, there is a little bit of blood. It wasn't a lot, but it was a little blood which made there was a tear or something. in the vagina.

So when that happened, she said, "You come in here, you come with me." She started me a bath and got a bath going and that's when she got the phone and let me call my mom. I called my mom and I told my mom what happened. My mom drove down there that same night and she came and got me.

Another time, she packed up all the grand kids for a trip to Nashville. We all piled into her station wagon—complete with that unique rear-facing back seat that let you watch the world disappear behind you. Carly was in that back seat while the rest of us filled the car.

At a gas station pit stop, my grandmother went inside, unaware that my sister KiKi had followed her out of the car.

The rest of us stayed put, waiting for her to return. Once my grandmother came back, she asked if everyone was ready, and off we went, merging onto the highway. Back then, there were no cell phones, only landlines and work beepers, which my grandmother had for emergencies.

As we pulled away, KiKi ran out of the gas station, waving her arms and yelling for us to stop. Carly and I, sitting in the back, found it amusing and waved back at her as if to say, "Bye, KiKi! See you later!" The car was filled with our usual road trip games, like reciting, "A is for apple, B is for ball, C is for cat," Goggy was oblivious to the fact that KiKi wasn't with us.

KiKi had to think fast. She managed to find someone at the gas station willing to help her call my grandmother's workplace, which then sent a page to her beeper. Eventually, my grandmother noticed the alert, pulled over, called back, and discovered that KiKi was left behind. We turned around to retrieve her, and while it was an unexpected detour, it became one of those stories that would make us all laugh for years to come.

My cousin Marissa lived with her mom in Dyersburg for a while, and one weekend, we went to visit them. Marissa's maternal grandparents, the Wadleys, were wealthy and owned a lot of land, complete with golf carts and other fun equipment. Her mom, Tina Wadley, had taken back her maiden name after divorcing my uncle Chris.

During our visit, everyone got a turn driving the golf carts, except for me. Being the youngest, they all insisted, "Amanda, You're too little. You can't even see over the steering wheel! It's too fast for you, and you wouldn't know what to do." Determined to prove them wrong, I waited for my chance. When everyone had stepped away, I turned the key and took off, only to crash and completely wreck the golf cart. From that moment, I was banned from visiting again, and we returned to my grandmother's house on Colonial Road.

Another unforgettable story involved Karen and Veronica being kidnapped when they were young by their father, Roger, who was Melissa's first husband. Roger, who passed away from cancer a couple of years ago, took them during a custody battle, though the exact details are hazy. It's believed that he picked them up from school and then disappeared with them.

While they were with him, they found ways to contact my grandmother. I remember my grandmother telling us how they once called her from a mall payphone in Nashville. My grandmother instructed them to put someone from the store on the line and to leave her number at a beeper station so they could stay in touch. She worked tirelessly, trying to buy beepers and cell phones to maintain communication and track them down.

Eventually, my grandmother's efforts paid off, and the situation went to court. My sister accompanied them, and the court granted full custody to my grandmother and aunt. Karen and Veronica came back home safely, and Roger never resurfaced in their lives: no child support, no visits, nothing. They didn't see him again until they were much older.

I attended Holy Rosary School until 3rd grade, then trans-ferred to St. Michael's for 4th and 5th grades. After that, I went to Ridgeway Middle School until 7th grade, before moving on to DeSoto Central Middle School. I continued at DeSoto Central through high school and graduated from there. After high school, I briefly attended Northwest Community College for one semester but ended up dropping out. Later on, I enrolled at Christian Brothers University (CBU).

In 4th grade, I was in Miss Brown's class at St. Michael's when the Twin Towers were hit on September 11th. I'll never forget the day. They announced over the intercom that school was being let out early, and students were being checked out. One of the kids in my class, named Chuck, was deeply affected by the events. His dad was impacted by what happened, and later on in life, Chuck tragically committed suicide. It was a devastating thing to learn.

When my grandmother lived in Mississippi, I was living there as well. My dad's mom, Edra, lived off Hacks Cross and Winchester, while we were in Nesbit, Mississippi. At this point, all of Goggy's grand kids, except for Marissa, lived with her. Marissa still lived with her mom and aunt, while KiKi and I stayed with my parents. Goggy lived in Olive Branch, and the house was a four-bedroom, two-bath with an open living area and a fenced-in backyard. It wasn't the same as the poolside house in Colonial, but we still had fun.

At this time, we were all getting older—around 14, 15, and 16—and had learned to drive. We didn't know many of the neighborhood kids because I went to school at DeSoto Central, while others went to Olive Branch High. We'd only see each other at football games. Veronica and Karen, however, went to school there and were close with their friends, many of whom had started smoking, drinking, and doing drugs.

I wasn't into that stuff yet. I just hung out with them, but soon enough, peer pressure got to me. One afternoon at Goggy's house, Veronica and I smoked together for the first time in the backyard. We were laughing about *The Fresh Prince of Bel-Air* and reminiscing about the good old days at Colonial.

The second time I smoked was in the garage with Veronica, Karen, and a friend of theirs. Karen gave me a shotgun, and it hit me so hard that I almost fell out of my seat and hit my head on the concrete. It was a wild experience that I'll never forget.

One night, Veronica and I snuck out to hang with her guy friends. One of them was driving a Tahoe, and as we were passing the railroad tracks near Goggy's, a train came barreling toward us. The driver panicked and tried to make a sharp U-turn, flipping the Tahoe over. We were stuck and scared, but one of the guys broke the sunroof to let us out. We walked back to Goggy's and snuck in quietly, hoping she wouldn't notice. But the next morning, she found blood on the floor and saw that Veronica was bruised. We had to explain the whole mess to her.

There were other crazy things that went down at Goggy's. My uncle Chris, who drove an 18-wheeler, had a serious drug problem. One day, Karen and I decided to break into his truck. We found Xanax and cash, so we took it and stashed it in the house, but that wasn't enough for us. We stole his truck and took it for a joyride around the neighborhood. Chris freaked out, calling us to return it, but we didn't care. We got back with the truck, and that was that.

There was also the time my friend stayed the night after a football game, and we snuck out to Goggy's again. We were just hanging out in the driveway when the police pulled up. They arrested us for breaking curfew and called Goggy to pick us up. When she found out, she was furious, but she refused to drive us back to our house. The police called her to notify her that they had picked up the teenagers. They informed there was a curfew. She informed them, matter of factly, that the kids had been in a car in her driveway, they were on private property, and that they were not breaking any curfew.

She told them, "You took them. You bring them back." And

36

the police did just that!

The next morning, she called my mom and told her every-thing. My mom was mad, and I was grounded for a while after that.

Even before all that happened, Veronica, Karen, and I used to sneak out late at night. We would wait until Goggy fell asleep, then roll her car down the driveway and drive around. We'd go to the trailer park to get weed, get high, and then sneak back in, all while Goggy had no idea what we were up to. That kind of stuff would never have flown at my mom's house, where she was always on top of things.

Despite all the chaos and mischief, Goggy's house remained the hub for everything. It was the party house, the hangout house—the place where everything seemed to happen.

4

Desoto Central High, Baby

During high school, I struggled to make friends. It was tough trying to fit in when I'd only spent one year in middle school, so most of the groups were already formed. I didn't have a specific group I hung out with; I was cool with everyone but never really part of any one clique. To be honest, high school wasn't great for me. My older sister, who had her own friends, let me hang out with her when she could, but most of the time, I was left to figure things out on my own. I bounced between different crowds, trying to find my place.

One group I spent time with was the "rocker" crowd, led by a girl named Cherish. Her family owned a lot of land, and that's where we'd throw bonfires. Those parties were crazy—people would be dropping acid, doing ecstasy, and even flipping over the fire. I remember one Halloween, I dressed as Cinderella, and we spent the day getting the place ready on four-wheelers, gathering beer, and paying older guys to run errands for us. It was wild, but it's how I got into the rock scene. Most of the guys at these parties were in bands, and I got to know them through their shows and the parties they threw.

One person who really stood out to me during this time was Freddy. He's been a genuine friend, never expecting anything in return, just always wanting to help me become the best version of myself. We formed a bond and he's always been in my corner as a friend, nothing more.

As for dating, I never really dated in high school. I usually dated older guys, but it was never anything serious. That changed during my 11th grade year when I met Cedric , the father of my first son. His brother was talking to one of my friends, and he told her to put me on the phone with him. From that moment on, I was hooked. When we met in person, it was like nothing else mattered—we were inseparable.

In high school, I struggled to pass my classes. No matter how hard I tried to study or learn the material, I just couldn't get it. So, I resorted to cheating. I didn't know the material, but I knew how to get by. Two teachers who really tried to help me were Tory Farmer, my math teacher, and Ashley Carter), my English teacher. They went above and beyond to support me, but despite their efforts, I still couldn't grasp the content. If it weren't for them, I probably never would have graduated.

Then there was this girl, Dancy. We didn't have a real friendship; it was transactional. She wanted Adderall, and I had been prescribed it but didn't use it. I quickly learned that people wanted it to help them focus and do their work, so I started selling it. Dancy was one of my regular customers, but instead of charging her full price, we worked out a deal since we always had the same class schedule. I'd sit behind her, and when we had a test, I'd cheat.

Before cell phones and cameras were everywhere, it was easier to get away with things. While Dancy took her test, I would just pretend to write something on mine, but I wouldn't actually put anything down. Then, I'd wait for her to finish and take her test. I'd cover her name with my arm, pretending to check my answers before turning it in. When it was time to hand in the tests, I'd turn mine in first, and then Nancy would follow, slipping her test at the bottom to avoid anyone noticing the answers were too similar. It worked out because if the teacher was distracted, it seemed like everything was normal.

For the big tests, though, the ones that counted, that's where the IEP (Individualized Education Plan) and tutoring came in. They'd basically give me the answers, just so they wouldn't have to deal with me again the next year. So, I passed high school not because I knew the material, but because I knew how to work the system. I'd sell the Adderall to get people to help me out, keep my homework done, and rely on tutoring to get through the big tests. As long as I kept up with my homework and projects, I knew I could pass. It was all about networking, doing favors, and knowing what I could offer someone in exchange for what I needed. I learned quickly that no one really cared about me personally—they just cared about what I could do for them.

A couple of people that I ran around with in high school were buying weed from this guy named E and one with my friends gave the number to Cedric but she wouldn't give the number to me. I'm guessing because she liked him and I later found out that she did. All the girls liked him. He was very attractive, very handsome, and he was on his shit. He had dope, he had money, cars, clothes, a job; he had everything going for him and to be honest he was easy on the eyes for me as well.

Cedric knew that and he got a feeling after we went to get weed a couple of times. He wouldn't give me the phone number and he would not let me meet E for weed or go to the door and pick it up. He would always make me sit in the car. I waited one night until Cedric got drunk and I got the number out for myself. I told E that I got the number from my home girl, which was a lie but I just needed an alibi. I looked for anyway to get in with him that I could.

As soon as I told him that, he was like "What's up?" which is means, "What are you trying to get?" I would tell him I'm just trying to get a gram or two. When I would come over, he would always make me feel so comfortable. We would hang out and then I would leave. We would do that a few times and I wouldn't let Cedric know because I felt like fuck him; all the shit that he does to me , the least I can do is being a guy's company and presence that valued me, enjoyed being there with me. After that I strictly started going to E myself to get weed because Cedric was trying to overcharge me so he could keep extra cash and get beer. I wouldn't know that until later when I found out the prices and shit.

5

Just Nickname Me Left Because We Will Never be Right

I met Cedric, my son Chase's dad, towards the end of 11th grade, and by the time 12th grade started, it was like everything shifted. I was obsessed with being around him, talking to him constantly. I didn't want to be anywhere else. My parents didn't approve, so I'd sneak around to see him. Skipping school became something we did often, especially because he was old enough to buy alcohol, and me and my friends wanted to drink. The whole situation was reckless, and I was so wrapped up in him that I barely focused on school. I almost didn't graduate, but somehow I managed to pull it together at the last minute.

I really thought we loved each other, but looking back, I think I loved him more than he loved me. To him, I was just an option, not the "chosen one." There was one point when I found out he'd been talking to another girl online, and things got messy. We'd fight, break up, and make up—again and again. Eventually, I got pregnant, and the first time I ended up getting an abortion. I was scared and didn't know what to do. I regretted it, but it happened.

When I did get the abortion, Planned Parenthood was taking any money they could get to do the abortions, no problem. What happened was they did do the abortion, but what they failed to tell me was I was too far along and they did it anyway. Once they did it and I went home, I didn't have a normal abortion. I was having bits and pieces, fingers, toes, a leg! I was having a dismembered baby come out in pieces! When I went to the hospital, we went to Saint Francis. I called my sister first and then she called my parents. I always called my sister first.

I also called Cedric to tell him I got the abortion but it went terribly fucking wrong. At that point we were fighting so bad he had another girl pick up the phone and tell me that they were having sex and he would call me back. He would do just about anything to just get me irate.

So at that point the doctor came in and said, "We're going to go ahead and and get the rest of the baby out."

I remember my sister being in the hallway and my mom and my dad standing behind my legs so that they were facing towards my vagina. The curtain was up and my face was on the other side, but I was looking up at my parents face to see how bad it was.

My mom turned to my dad and put her hands over her face and said, "Alan, I can't take it" and he had to hold her and walk her out of the room because the baby was so badly dismembered.

Originally, I wasn't told that, I was just simply given an abortion pill and told me that I was just gonna have a few blood clots and it just absolutely wasn't the case out. I had to get a blood transfusion after and it put me down. Cedric and I were arguing so bad after my blood transfusion at Saint Francis, they threatened to put me in the psych ward on the bottom floor because of all of the threats that was going back and forth. When my sister came by and saw me with her boyfriend Mike, at the time, I took my own IV out and I told him to pull the car around. I walked right out behind them; he was bigger so I could hide behind him as we walked. We left that night went to Taco Bell and I got a Mexican pizza with no beans and extra meat; I'll never forget it

Another thing I will never forget is my aunt Melissa giving me and my sister the money for the abortion. The reason I can't forget it is she because she throws it in my face. I love her, but it hurts me every time she does it. It was one of the most horrific events of my life and she won't let me or my mom forget it. Out of spite, Melissa always brings it up to my mom that I went to her instead; that I didn't trust my mom enough. She brags about it to the point it has really affects mine and my mom's relationship. The funny thing is, my mom took her and her kids in when she needed it. My mom provided for her big sister and her kids, no questions asked. This continual beratement from my aunt is probably one of the reasons my mom has the emotional pain that she does. It is a constant sibling rivalry.

The second time I got pregnant, I knew I wasn't going to do it again. I couldn't go through that pain, so I decided to keep the baby. The first phone call I made was to NeNe, crying telling her the news while explaining the situation. With her already knowing about the previous pregnancy, she quickly told me if I wanted to keep my baby I could do this. I could keep it and be the best mom ever.

She told me, "Don't feel alone for one second because I would always have her. I'm serious Amanda. i will be here for you."

After I got off the phone with NeNe, I went downstairs to tell my mom. Scared and shaking, but with the confidence that NeNe had given me, I was able to confront my mother. When I told my mom, she was supportive, and we went to my grandmother's house to tell her. It was a bit awkward, but she was happy and gave me a hug. My cousin, Karen, who had a rough home life and was planning an abortion herself, then surprised everyone by saying she was pregnant, too, and wanted to keep her baby as well. It felt like she was trying to take the attention away from me, which hurt.

Karen and I ended up having our babies a month apart. Her baby was born in October, and mine in November. I had already planned my baby shower, and when she found out, she tried to steal my date. My mom made her change hers to the week before mine. It was a weird competition, and it always felt like she was trying to overshadow me.

When I had Chase, things started to shift. My parents started accepting Cedric more, especially after my mom helped him get his GED so he could have better opportunities. She even used money from a tax return to buy him a truck, believing that we needed stability if we were going to have a family, but I was still so young and naive. I didn't realize how bad Cedric's behavior was—he just wanted to party, drink, and be loud. I thought it was attractive, but now I know it wasn't at all.

I was working at FedEx where I met Lucy while Cedric was working at Budget Care rentals. so we could have us an apartment in McKellar Woods off Airways Blvd. and Holmes Rd, being my parents and his dad were in Mississippi. We worked off Democrat Rd. It made sense that we lived in the middle. I was introduced to Lucy's family when I was going to Riverside in South Memphis. I met her family, Mama May and Papa May, her nephew Terry, her brother Robert, and her baby, Michael. They were all living in this one house off of Swift Road and that is when the relationship between me and Terry sparked up. That was a whole other situation.

When I found out I was pregnant again, it all just came crashing down. One night after an argument, I had had enough. Cedric said he was leaving, and I couldn't accept it. I packed up Chase and left with him. We stayed with my parents, and I started working at FedEx. Cedric and I went back and forth—arguing, breaking up, and then making up.

One day, when he went to Budget. I decided to take action. I was just done. I was just I was fucking done. I was at my lowest. I was pregnant and working the night shift, and he wasn't even picking me up from my job. I was having to walk home. He was trying to put his hands on me. He was arguing with me, cussing me out, and I had just had it. I had had it to the point I set the apartment on fire. My pregnancy had me so full of rage. I started a fire and I laid down for a second. I was just going to get back up; I was just going to burn just a little part of the apartment and put it out just to tell him, more like warn him, I'll set this whole shit on fire. In reality I ended up setting the everything on fire. I must have fallen asleep because of the smoke; all I remember is the next door neighbors busting down the door to rescue me. After they got me out, that's when I called Cedric and told him the apartment burned down, but I knew damn well that I set it on fire and that it was not by accident. I knew what I did and how I did it. Because of this, we had to move to my parents' house and it lead to the argument that caused him to move to his cousin's house. I was staying at my mom's house. We continued to go back and forth with me really just chasing him after he got with me, and then I had the baby.

He never had to chase me or put much effort into the relationship because he felt like he already had me. It was always me doing the chasing, making all the plans and arrangements. I had the car, the responsibility—it was all on me. Meanwhile, he was constantly in and out of jail. It wasn't a healthy situation, and I couldn't get him to change. I thought maybe having Chase would make him shift his priorities, but it only made things worse. His behavior just kept spiraling, and no matter how hard I tried to make a family work, nothing changed.

After I had Chase, living in Mississippi, it became clear that something had to give. Cedric got locked up and was sentenced to ten years, though he ended up serving only five. I remember going to visit him in Hernando, walking all the way there and back from Nesbitt. It was during that three hour walk when I realized something—this chapter was over. There was no fixing it. I had to do something for myself, for my son. The relationship was done, and I finally understood that it was time to move on.

After seeing him in jail, I knew it was over. This wasn't what I wanted, and definitely not what I deserved. Even with Chase in the picture, I realized I could do better—I just didn't know how. At that point, I had been to jail myself for a minor marijuana possession charge. I had some court dates and fines in Mississippi that I couldn't take care of, and I was just fed up. I remember going to jail once, and Cedric, who I had bailed out multiple times, couldn't even help me. He couldn't be bothered, yet I had been there for him every time. It became clear on the walk back from visitation—this was over. I had to do something for myself, if not for myself. at least my son.

I was on probation and I kept failing a drug test. I went to rehab for drugs, but there was no drugs in my system. The first time I went to La Paloma my dad dropped me off and got the insurance to pay for it because somehow I could not stop smoking marijuana to pass a drug test for the charges that I was up against. I ended up doing what any celebrity would do; I ran to the nearest and most fabricated rehab I could find, the most plushest one that would accommodate me to my every needs even down to days on Wednesday when we would go and have hair and nail day.

People there asked me, "Why are you here?"

I answered, "I went crazy. That's why I went to jail because of it and I got put on probation because of my baby's father. That's why I'm here and I can't pass. I can't keep passing the drug screens because I smoke marijuana."

They asked, "Marijuana? That's it? So you are in here for being crazy, like mental, like obsession. PTSD."

I went to La Paloma because that is a dual diagnosis rehab, and they basically diagnosed me with. PTSD and bipolar. I don't think I always had bipolar. I think I developed it with this shit that I've been through that triggers me and that also stems from PTSD and all of the things.

It was him. Making me think he loves me and he doesn't. Making me think that I should do things for him and he doesn't do things for me. He would just play with my head and the whole time he had a whole another relationship, and come to find out he ended up having three kids with with the Atlanta girl in Ohio. It was all fucked up in some type of way because of his drinking problem.

You would think I had learned my lesson, but things got complicated when Cedric came back into the picture. One day, Cedric, my aunt Tina (who is Marissa's mom), and I were in the car. Tina needed Lortab, and Cedric knew where to get them, but he had no car. I had the car, but no money or connections, so we all went together. Unfortunately we got pulled over and busted. I was the only one who ended up in jail because I was driving. Tina dropped Cedric off and went back to my grandmother's house like nothing happened. She didn't even tell anyone I had gone to jail; the only reason anyone knew was because I had to call from the Olive Branch Detention Center.

6

Hillview

When I got transferred to Hernando, Cedric once again couldn't help me. He was too busy figuring out where his next beer or fix was coming from. While I was in jail, I met a girl named KC. We were the only two white girls in there who weren't on drugs or completely out of it. We became fast friends, and we made a pact that whoever got out first would help the other. Her charges were minor, so I knew she'd get out before me. She had connections, and I had some ideas, too, thanks to my aunt's history.

By this point, I was dating a guy named Maine Maine. We were talking, but it wasn't official. We were exclusive in the sense that neither of us talked to anyone else, but there was no label.

One day, while talking to him in the Oakshire apartments, I asked, "Are we dating, or what's going on? KC brings me over here every day to see you, we hang out, and we have a good time. What are we doing?"

At this point, I had already signed temporary custody of Chase to my parents because, while I was in jail, there was no one else to take care of him. My parents took him in, and I was crashing wherever I could—either with KC or Maine Maine.

He said, "Yeah, You're with me," and after that, I didn't leave. I stayed with him wherever he went.

Maine Maine was selling drugs in Hillview, but I quickly learned it wasn't his weed. He would have to go get it from someone else and never let me meet the people he dealt with. But one day, I had to use the bathroom, and when I knocked on the door, a big guy answered. He was confused, asking why I was there.

I explained, and he said, "You're with Maine Maine, right?" Turns out, he was the stepdad of a friend, Tim Tim, and he was the one running the show. He took a cut off the prices just for knowing me, which Maine Maine appreciated. Things started moving fast after that.

Life in Oakshire became routine: we'd drink, smoke, get food, clean up, and do it all over again. It was like living in a trap house. People came and went, and though Maine Maine wasn't deep into hard drugs, he was doing cocaine behind my back, which I didn't find out about until later. Eventually, Oakshire apartments got shut down, and we had to find a new place.

Maine Maine's dad had a history—he killed Maine Maine's mom and staged it to look like a suicide so he could be with another woman. Maine Maine's dad had left her, and she was the one who ended up raising Maine Maine. So, when we needed a place to stay, Maine Maine took me to his dad's ex-girlfriend's house. We went into the backroom to talk, and when he came out, he told me to grab my stuff. I wasn't exactly thrilled about it, but I had no other choice. We'd been staying there, but there wasn't a room for us. We had to sleep on the couch, but at least we had somewhere to go.

I kept in touch with Lucy, but I didn't tell her everything. I just told her the basics, like, "Yeah, I'm living with Maine Maine now, we're in Hillview, and he sells weed, so let me know if I need some." But things quickly went downhill from there.

Living in Hillview was a completely different reality for me. To be honest, it felt like a small piece of land, overrun with people scrambling for anything—just trying to survive. I always used to think of it as a place where everyone was just scavenging, hustling for a quick dollar or looking for something to do to get by. If anyone asked where I lived, I'd never say Hillview. I'd say I was in "The Walking Penitentiary," because it felt like being surrounded by danger, where a charge was waiting to happen at any moment—whether it was someone trying to rob you or even worse, take your life. The tension was constant, and anything that could go wrong, would, and it would happen there. I had to learn the ropes fast or risk getting caught in the chaos.

At first, things seemed okay when we got there. He had a brother named Popcorn, who I thought was gay—something that came out later—and a younger brother, Tonka, who was naïve, always trying to prove himself, but never quite making it. Tonka ended up dying later. He also had a sister, Mercedes, who I thought would eventually turn straight, have a kid, and then return to her partner. Turns out, that's exactly what happened. Tiffany, their mom, called all the shots. She would try to put me on the game, making sure I had money in my pocket, but I didn't always realize what was happening. She'd tell me it was to help me, but sometimes, I wondered if I could have just gotten a job instead.

Hillview was dangerous. Everyone had a gun, even the

women, and if they didn't, they had tricks or hidden routes to escape if things went south. If I weren't from there, I wouldn't know where to go if someone tried to rob you, and they'd get away with it. I watched and adapted, but deep down, I was shocked by what I saw. Still, when I thought about it, I couldn't judge these people. They were just doing what they had to do to survive, just like me. I realized that what I thought about them was the same as what others might think about me, not understanding my situation.

Tiffany ruled the house. People went to her room for everything—payments, arrangements, or just trying to figure out how to get out of a bind. Maine Maine said everything would be fine as long as we were together, and we'd make it work. I did my part: cleaning, cooking, and contributing what I could, but things only got worse over time. When he drank, he became mean, possessive, and violent. He'd get upset if I even spoke to someone. One time, someone came to the door asking for him, and I simply responded, but he immediately pulled me into the kitchen questioning why I spoke to them.

We lived in an apartment in Hillview, right on the corner, downstairs while his family lived upstairs. Their place was busy too, with constant traffic from people trying to buy drugs or shoot dice. Sometimes, gunshots rang out right at our doorstep. It got so bad that I had to put a sign up: "After 11 PM, You have to spend $50 or we won't open the door." Maine Maine would get pills and try to sell anything he could get his hands on. The constant flow of people and drugs made everything feel like a never-ending cycle of survival, and I couldn't escape it.

Hillview was a place where survival wasn't just about getting by—it was about adapting to a harsh reality, doing whatever I could to stay afloat, even if it meant becoming someone I didn't recognize. Before we got to Hillview, when we were still in Oakshire, none of the terrible things had started yet. There were small signs, little hints, but I ignored them. I didn't see the full picture. By the time we moved to Hillview, everything escalated. That's when it became obvious that Maine Maine felt untouchable. There was no one to tell him what to do, no one to stop him, and he took full advantage of that—especially with me. It wasn't okay, but I felt powerless.

The situation escalated when he started using the house as a trap house, selling anything and everything he could. He'd trade drugs for items like TVs, or whatever else people would bring in. He didn't care; his focus was on the transactions. I learned a lot about how it all worked—what drugs were what prices, and the dynamics of it all. But as things progressed, his behavior got more abusive. There were countless times I couldn't even remember the exact details, just the feeling of it. Once, I was beaten so badly that I had to curl into a fetal position, covering my head, trying to protect myself. Tiffany, his mom, came out and told him if he was going to beat me like that, he should do it outside because she didn't want to hear it.

There was another time when he was coming down from a drug high, and he took his anger out on me, being extremely possessive. If I had anything—money, a car—he'd take it. My mom, Evelyn, would come over, but instead of bringing money, she'd take me to Walmart, buy me a mini-fridge, and stock it with groceries so I wouldn't go hungry. They were using my food stamps, eating everything, and I still had nothing. The abuse kept getting worse, and one night it was over something small: I ate the last plate of food, not realizing it was for Tiffany. That night, I was beaten again, and this time Mercedes, his sister, came out and told him to stop. He snapped at her, telling her she wasn't even there for her own kid, but Mercedes stepped in and pulled me into her room, locking the door so he couldn't hurt me anymore.

Things didn't get any better. At one point, there was a party in Hillview, and I got accused of stealing a phone just because I was sitting near where it went missing. Everyone at the party turned on me, calling me a thief, and he beat me in the car all the way home. When we got back to the apartment, I thought the beating was over, but it wasn't. He waited until I was about to shower, then dragged me outside, naked, in front of a crowd of people. He kicked and punched me, my hair yanked as he dragged me out. Thankfully, some people, including my smoking buddy, Amp and my upstairs neighbor Carlysia, witnessed it and tried to intervene. They called Hammer, another guy who sold drugs in the area, and they managed to cover me with a sheet. He confronted my abuser, telling him that wasn't the right way to treat a woman, and eventually helped get me inside Carlysia's place to safety.

The next day, when I thought I'd be left alone, he came knocking, apologizing and telling me he didn't think I had stolen the phone. I was stupid enough to go back with him, walking down three flights of stairs on my own, even though he didn't help me. Tiffany moved out, and then Mercedes and I got our own room, with the den becoming the "trap." I was trying to push myself to work, and I eventually got a job at Olive Garden, though I still kept in touch with Lucy, who was a true friend and helped me escape when I needed it.

It was a toxic situation. He would cheat on me constantly, which was why I never felt guilty when I was with someone else. I never had multiple partners, unlike him. One time, we were fighting over this bitch he invited over to serve some coke, and I wouldn't stand for it, so he called the police on me, and I was terrified of going to jail. I couldn't stand the thought of being stuck there with no one to bail me out. So, I acted crazy, did everything I could to make sure they didn't take me to jail. When they got to the holding area, I made a scene, hoping they'd take me somewhere else, and it worked. I was sent to Lakeside instead, which felt like my only option. It was a facility that wasn't based on money, so I figured if I played my cards right, I could get out of there without staying stuck for good.

While I was there, we had a phone that allowed us to call, but it only lasted for a few minutes. It was free, though, so I'd call as much as I could. That was my escape from the chaos.

Maine Maine was doing the same thing as Cedric did, but with Maine Maine it was more physical. Cedric was never a physical, maybe twice, but that was it and then I left. Maine Maine was physical because I was stuck. I couldn't go back. There was no going back. I couldn't go anywhere else. With Maine Maine, it was physically, spiritually, emotionally, and psychologically. All of the things were just abused. It was just abuse so bad.

I reached a point where I was talking to Lucy about getting away—just to escape the mental abuse. I knew that if I went to her house, I wouldn't be hit or woken up by being kicked over small things like not emptying the mop water or not turning on the kitchen light. At Lucy's house, her parents treated me like family. They loved me unconditionally, something I wasn't getting at home. I felt cared for there, like I mattered.

During that time, I had gotten involved with KC, who was working at a furniture store by day and selling sex at night. I never participated in the tricks, but I helped as security, staying in the car while she worked. A couple of times, she suggested

I get involved to make more money, and I did, but I never felt comfortable. KC and I had an arrangement, but things got complicated when she started bringing in a lot more money than I was. I couldn't get a regular job without a car, so I started considering doing what KC did to survive.

Eventually, Lucy gave me tough love, telling me that nothing in life comes free, and that I had to figure out a way to support myself. I was stuck, and though I didn't want to, I ended up doing some of the things KC was doing. By the time I was at Hillview, KC had her own situation with her boyfriend, Bird, and was doing her thing while I focused more on Lucy. But even when we were all still connected, I kept everything compartmentalized, using names for people based on where I met them or where they were from. It helped me keep my distance emotionally, which is how I got through it.

I remember staying at Lucy's house and Maine Maine showing up, refusing to leave until he talked to me. I'll never forget this one time, where we were in the back room of Lucy's house. He was trying to abuse me, trying to make me leave and come back to him in Hillview. They heard the fighting, and my Mama May went back there, armed with a knife. Maine Maine put the knife to his neck, the skin just about breaking but not yet.

She said, "You better get your hands off my daughter, do you understand me?"

Then Papa Lee came in behind her, saying, "May, put the knife down, what are you doing?"

May fired back, "You better not do nothing or I'll kill you, you hear me? Leave her the hell alone, stop putting your hands on her."

Papa Lee stepped in between them, telling May, "Go inside. Go sit in the front room."

Then he sat in front of me and Lucy and said, "I think it's best you go ahead and leave now. You go on and walk out while you can, because you might not be able to walk out that door much longer."

That's when he left, but he kept calling me. He'd call over and over, playing the narcissist card, saying, "This is your fault. You put yourself in this situation. You could be here with me, living good, not sleeping on a couch. You could have your own room." Just all the same manipulation, all the narcissistic things he would say.

Maine Maine bought me everything—outfits, pads, panties, bras, clothes—anything I had was because he bought it. The only reason I had food was because my mother bought it. That was the situation. But still, I kept going back. No matter how bad it got, no matter where I went or how long I stayed at Lucy's or anyone else's, I always ended up back at Mama May's or Papa Lee's house. It didn't matter if I had to sleep on the couch. I'd rather be safe, be loved by people who actually cared about me, than go back and get beaten every single day. There were so many times I stayed at Lucy's, trying to get away. I stayed there for months, trying to leave him, but I was always stuck in that cycle.

The entire experience was a roller coaster of ups and downs, but throughout it all, Lucy and her family were my rock. They were always there for me with an open door and kind words, no matter how many times I stumbled. My own family, on the other hand, failed to show up for me in ways they should have, no matter how many times I reached out.

There was a time when Maine Maine had been up partying for days with people in the house—smoking, drinking, and likely using something stronger. I didn't really know what was going on, since I'd usually be asleep, but one day when he came home, he told me to clean up the dishes we'd just eaten from. I said no. I was fed up with being pushed around, and I told him, "I can't do it. I've cooked, cleaned, and done everything else."

His response was pure anger. "What did you just say to me?" he snapped. I repeated myself, even though I was scared. I was so tired of being bullied. And that's when it all escalated. He hit me and knocked me to the floor. When I tried to get up, he hit me again. Then, he sat on my torso and pressed his knees onto my arms so I couldn't move. He had a cigarette in his hand, and in that moment, he burned my face twice—once on each side. I was in shock, screaming in pain, but no one was there to help.

He got off me eventually, telling me to go wash my face. But when I looked in the mirror, seeing the burns on my face, I couldn't stop crying. It wasn't about the scarring; it was the searing pain that hit me every time I moved my face. The only relief I could find was by pressing cold rags against my skin. Later, he came in, pretending to be remorseful. "I'm sorry, you can't talk to me like that. I'm sorry, baby," he said. He even offered to get me food, but I couldn't eat. I couldn't even speak without it hurting. I took myself to the hospital. They wanted to make a police report, so I did, but with falsified information. If he left what would I do; where would I go.

That was one of the moments I came close to leaving. But the reality was, I didn't have anywhere to go. My family wasn't a reliable option. I didn't want to go back to Lucy's house; I felt like a burden, and I didn't want to keep imposing on anyone. So I stayed, despite the pain, despite everything.

There was another time when things got even worse. He had gotten upset because I refused to continue selling my body and stripping for money. I told him I was done, that I'd get a job, which eventually led me to working at Olive Garden. He didn't like it, though. He needed me to make money, and when I wouldn't, he found someone else.

One day, he came back to the apartment with a woman and two small kids. She was homeless, and he had made arrangements with her.

She came in, kids in tow, and he told me, "She's gonna work for me. And if you're not gonna work for me, she will."

I was furious. Everything I did, everything I gave, and it was never enough. But this—this crossed the line. It was one of the worst moments, realizing that he had no regard for my dignity, and that he was using someone else the same way he'd used me.

He took the woman in the back and left me in the front of the apartment with the kids. He left me up there with the kids and I didn't say shit. I started getting bolder and bolder over time. At this point I didn't give a fuck if I went to jail because if I went to jail, at least he couldn't beat me there and I could sleep there for free. I could get a free meal, and peace of mind. Hell, to be honest, jail sounded like a vacation to me.

If you go down to the women's shelter, you have to be there at a certain time. You have to get kicked out at a certain time. They only have a certain amount of beds. There's mold in the facility, so that wasn't an option. I'd rather just keep getting my ass beaten, going through what I was going through, then having to go through that on the street and really not having anywhere to go. What if I missed the line? What if there wasn't enough beds and I was there on time? Where would I go to? Back to Lucy's house, then I would be their problem once again, every time. That is what it led back to, I would have to go back and be a burden to them.

So I was watching the two babies, but I took them with me and I walked up to the store and got gasoline. I didn't know what I was going to do with the gasoline. I just know that I was going to burn this fuck out of him, her, somebody, somebody had to pay for this shit. Why did she think that? That was OK just to come in? Like he laid some rules down, like he's a pimp, like he's somebody he's not. But I don't know, maybe she was fucked up, too, and in a position where she didn't know what to do either. So I had both of her babies and in Hillview, the nearest gas station is Shell on Airways and Ketchum. I walked with both babies that weren't mine to the gas station to get gas and came back. I went upstairs. I sat the babies down in the den. I ran upstairs. They weren't my babies, so I didn't care if something happened to them, just as long as nothing killed them. I set them down in the den, knowing that nothing would happen because I'm running upstairs real quick.

I went upstairs and ran in to Carlysia and told her, "Maine Maine just brought this bitch home with two kids from the store. He said he's gotta go back there to fuck her to see how much his her pussy's worth. They come back and she's gonna start working for him because I can't get a job right now. I'm still swollen; I'm still beat up. How in the hell do you expect me to work?"

She said, "So you went and got gas."

I said, "Yeah," and kind of laughed.

And she said, "Girl, you're fucking crazy. He sees that gas, he's gonna go crazy. What the hell did you think you were doing?"

I said, "I don't know Carlysia. I'm so fucking mad." I was crying. "I know I can't hit him. He's going to beat me up. I know if I fight her, she probably beat my ass, too. In my condition,

I can't fight. I can't even take up for myself, so I need to do something. Nobody else can take up or or will take up for me. So I got to do something."

She was like, "Yeah. I guess you're right about that here. You're going to need this."

I asked, "What? A Windex bottle?"

She said, "No, girl, take the Windex out and put the gas in the bottle. Whoever you decide to catch on fire, put that gasoline in that bottle. Spray it down and then light them on fire. That way it doesn't spill or leak on you. That big ass gasoline can, as soon as you stop pouring, it's still going to leak the trail."

She was right and I didn't think about that, but the only thing she didn't tell me was you only have a certain amount of time before the gas burns through the plastic. So I poured it in there. She walked out.

I called out, "Hey, Maine Maine, we need to go to the store because we don't have shit in the house. I need to get bread and stuff if they're going to be here, we need food."

He was like, "Alright, alright, let her go with you so y'all can get to know each other."

I was like, "OK, that's cool."

So she grabbed her kids and she put them in the truck. I acted like I was getting in the driver's seat, but then I got out and I popped the trunk, acting like I was looking for something in the trunk. I wasn't looking for shit. I had already put everything I needed in the trunk. She didn't think anything of it. She was thinking I was just checking out the car because we're about to go. Maybe we needed space for groceries. No, that's not what was going on at all. She set the two kids down, and as soon as she shut the back door, I sprayed that bitch with the gas and lit the match on fire! Her hair lit up first and then it got to her

62

scalp. Then she and Maine Maine started patting her clothes to put fire out.

Maine Maine yelled, "What the fuck is wrong with you?"

I screamed, "What the fuck is wrong with you? What would make you think you're going to bring a hoe to this house; like you just going to pimp some hoes out of here? What the fuck do you think this is?

"You got me pissed off," he said.

"Maine Maine, give me the keys to the car," I said, so he gave the keys to the car. Come to find out as soon as he got done patting her out, he dropped the keys when he ran in the car.

I said, "Bitch, get in the fucking car!" She got in the car. I dropped her ass off all the way in North Memphis. I dropped her and those kids at the Marathon off of Hollywood. I drove all the way back to Hillview and he was sitting there just cussing me out, but he never put a fucking hand on me that day. He never put a hand on me because he knew I had that fucking gas.

Things kept getting worse, and I finally decided I couldn't take it anymore. One day, I started packing my things, getting ready to leave. I remember Messay, his sister, and Melissa, his brother's girlfriend, both saw me packing. When Melissa opened the door and saw what I was doing, she said, "Girl, he's gonna kill you." I was terrified, but I knew I couldn't stay anymore. So I called Lucy and told her I was leaving. She promised to help me, but I had to sneak out.

We had to be careful. I couldn't leave through the front door; he watched everything. Lucy and her nephew came to help, and they pulled up behind the apartment, where my window was. I handed out all my belongings through the window—clothes, a refrigerator, shoes. It was like a scene out of a movie, but it was real. By the time he came home from work, I was already gone. I left everything behind, even some of his stuff, because I felt like I deserved it.

I took what I could, pawned some of it to get by, and left for good. I had no plan but to survive, hoping that somehow, I'd figure it out. I stayed at Papa Nick and Mama May's place, but I still had to face the hard truth of having to tell them.

When I finally gathered the courage, I went inside and spoke to her. "Mama May," I said, "I need to talk to you."

I remember going to her to talk about everything that was happening. Before I could even get the words out, she answered for me.

She said, "Yes, she talks to me. What do you think you're doing in here? She's gotta talk to you too, but we both have to say it." She went on, "I don't have a problem with you coming home. This is your home, girl. You can always come here. You don't have to ask. Get your stuff off the porch and bring it inside."

I moved back in with them just to get away from Maine Maine. I wanted him to know that I could leave anytime, that I wasn't stuck. When he worked, I would go out. I didn't have friends or anyone to really hang with, but I knew the people he talked to. I talked to his family—his aunt, Amp, Hammer, and a few others. Amp knew Hammer, and Hammer had the real stuff, the kind that came straight from the source, uncut, no nonsense. If Amp didn't have anything, we had to go to Hammer, though his prices were always crazy high. But Hammer's stuff? It was top-tier, no question.

Just as before with Cedric, I found myself continuing to revisit my past. Though I had left Maine Maine for awhile, it wasn't long before I returned to him. Back in Hillview, when Maine Maine went to work, that was my chance to get out. I spent a lot of time hanging around with Amp. He was the one who let everyone know I was cool. My aunt, Melissa, had a guy named Javier come over once. He was supposed to be a client, but Melissa stole from him. He got angry and refused to work with her again, but he ended up being someone I could trust. Javier became like an uncle to me. He always gave people a chance, but everyone ended up taking advantage of him—except me. We got close, and I could depend on him, and he could depend on me.

Melissa lost her job because of her addiction. She was deep into crack, and it started to show. We'd see her post ads on Craigslist, and she'd get us to go to hotels while she was upstairs doing God knows what. We didn't fully understand it when we were kids, but we knew something was off. When we were older, it all clicked. She'd have us play in the pool or just stay out of sight while she did what she needed to do to make money. She'd flash cash, showing us how much she made, buying us things, and telling us to run errands like getting liquor. It was transactional, just like her sister, my mom. I think that's where my mom learned it.

She wasn't just doing her thing in Memphis—she was going to Ohio, Florida, Arkansas, all over. When she lost her job, she dove into crack and prostitution. She even got her daughters involved. They did the same thing, selling themselves for money. Even though they've probably stopped now, it always stayed in the back of their minds that if they ever needed money, they could always fall back on that lifestyle. It was a reality— fast money, a way to survive when I felt like I had no other option.

Javier was a mechanic, and even though he was a great guy, I never understood why people treated him so badly. He was always willing to help, always had your back, but people just took from him, but I didn't do that. He trusted me, and I never betrayed that trust. He would help me out when I needed it—whether it was fixing cars or supplying me with weed. I'd call him up and ask if I could sell some of it, and he'd front me the product. I would sell it, pay him back, and keep the profit. That's when I learned how to make money without putting myself on the line with men. I started selling drugs, and from that point, I never had to go back to doing anything else.

I was stuck in a toxic situation, unable to escape the cycle of abuse. There were days I didn't know where my next meal was coming from, or where I'd sleep at night. I'd try to figure out a way to survive, but my options were always limited. I couldn't tell my family what I was going through—there was no point. They'd just judge me, as always. So I kept to myself, pushing through the pain, surviving the best I could, and praying every night. My grandmother's advice to pray gave me some peace, even though my situation seemed hopeless.

She said, "It doesn't matter what you're going through just to pray. God." She always believed in prayer. And that's mainly what I did every time he would beat my ass or every time I would think I would hear the door open and he come from work. Every time I would think he was coming in or going out. I would pray, "Please don't let him beat my ass. Please don't let me beat my ass." I would try to see how many Hail Marys I could say and. how fast I could say them. I would think to myself, "How fast could I say the Hail Mary within 5 minutes? How many did could I say?

There were moments I questioned everything, including how I was living and what I was doing. I found myself constantly trying to get out of a toxic environment, but it felt like there was no way out. I had no resources, no one to turn to—except a priest I met who, instead of offering money, gave me food and a book about saints, a dictionary of the different ones and the situations they help with, It helped me find strength in prayer. That book became a lifeline, teaching me how to focus my energy on something bigger than my pain. I still have it to this day.

Things got worse when my abuser started bringing other women around, and I felt trapped. I tried to find a way out by focusing on anything else—anything to keep my mind off the fear and the anger. I walked miles just to get gas, with no real plan, just the desire to do something that would make it all stop.

In the end, I was at a breaking point. My frustration led me to an extreme reaction, trying to fight back in the only way I thought would matter at that moment. The situation escalated, but somehow, despite the rage and the chaos, he didn't hurt me that day. I was exhausted and broken, but for the first time, I felt like I had control over something.

Maine Maine had just bought a truck, a blue Ford Explorer, but it kept breaking down. He was constantly under the hood trying to fix it. Finally, after a lot of effort, he managed to get it running. But things got tense again—he hit me in the back of my head, and I fell forward, hurting my left eye. This wasn't the first time something like this had happened. Once again, I found myself in a situation where I couldn't fight back. I couldn't hurt him with my words, because that would only lead to more violence. And physically, I knew I couldn't win. No matter what I did or said, I was at his mercy.

By this time, I had moved out of the apartment and had gone back to Lucy's house for a couple of months, trying to get some space. Before I left, I had been talking to Chicago, someone I had been seeing on the sly. I told him I was done with everything—the drugs, the money, all of it. I just wanted to stop. I had a small amount of weed I was selling, but I needed something more to get by. That's when he suggested heroin. I wasn't sure, but I went along with it.

I knew a girl named Sharyn, who came from a wealthy family. Her father had owned a catfish company, but after he passed away, she spiraled into addiction. She had a lot of money once, but it all disappeared as she became consumed by drugs. Now, she was homeless, bouncing from place to place, still looking for a way to get high. When I connected with her, we'd trade drugs—if I had something, she'd help me out with what I needed.

Chicago told me he knew someone who could get heroin, but he didn't know how to test it, so, I told him I'd bring Sharyn along. She was the one who knew what to look for. I wasn't going to pay for anything until we knew the quality. We met in a hotel room, and sure enough, once Sharyn hit the heroin, her whole demeanor changed. She was out in minutes—completely gone, her eyes rolled back. I explained to Chicago that this meant the heroin was good. When she was that high, it was a clear sign that it was strong.

From there, I began selling the heroin, getting it from Chicago and making money by moving it. But it wasn't something I had ever done before—my previous partner didn't know the ropes of dealing or even what the drug went by. He didn't understand how it worked. I had to step in and handle it, getting the drugs out there and making the money I needed to survive.

At this point, I'm running around Hillview, trying to stay on top of things. For the past 2 or 3 years, Maine Maine had been beating me up, and now, I had finally gained some respect—not from him, but from others. Once people found out that I had the drugs, everything shifted. Maine Maine, who used to have control, was suddenly seen as weak, and people didn't want anything to do with him. They wanted to come straight to me. But I couldn't let that happen directly, so I had to figure out who I could trust to help me.

One time, when Maine Maine and I were in Hillview, something happened that escalated everything. Someone came by to buy a dime bag, and I gave it to them. Later, they came back for two grams, so I grabbed a bag from Maine Maine's stash, thinking it was two grams like they asked. I didn't know that the bag I handed them was actually three grams. Maine Maine had pre-bagged everything himself; I didn't weigh it out or mess with it. But when he found out what happened, he lost it.

Maine Maine beat me so badly that I ended up in the hospital for a week. My eye was swollen shut, and I was on oxygen because I couldn't breathe properly. It was so severe that I was in the ICU in critical condition. When I woke up, I could barely move—my jaw throbbed, and swallowing felt like agony. I couldn't talk, but when I opened my eyes, Sharyn was sitting there in a chair next to me.

She leaned forward and said, "It's me, friend. You don't have to talk. I know he did this to you."

All I could do was nod, tears streaming down my face. She grabbed my hand and said, "Don't worry, girl. We're going to get him. If it takes everything in me, I'm not going to let him touch you again."

I smiled through the pain because I knew Sharyn meant it with her whole heart. But deep down, we both knew the truth:

there wasn't much we could do. And worse, we knew that once I was discharged from the hospital, I'd have to go back to him.

Sure enough, when it was time for me to leave, guess who came to pick me up? Maine Maine. I didn't have anyone else to turn to. I didn't have a safe place to go, and I desperately needed the pain medicine the hospital prescribed because I couldn't even chew or swallow without unbearable pain. It hurt to do anything, even breathe. So I got in the car with the same man who had just put me in the ICU.

I was so desperate for a way out, I would try anything. Maine Maine controlled everything, including my phone, so I couldn't contact anyone. When people came by, he thought I was in our room, but I'd sit in the hallway instead, waiting for a chance to ask someone for help.

I'd beg people, "Can I use your phone? Please, I just need to make one call."

But they'd always refuse. They'd say, "I'm not getting in the middle of whatever y'all got going on." No one wanted to risk it, especially since Maine Maine was always coked up and unpredictable.

One time, he took my phone for two weeks. For three days, I begged anyone who came by, but no one would let me use their phone. Eventually, I started telling people, "I just need to check on my son, please." That seemed to work occasionally. They'd go into the bathroom, let me use their phone, and then knock on Maine Maine's door.

When I did get the chance to call, I'd keep it short. I'd tell Lucy, "I'm okay. He has my phone, but I don't know how long this will last. I'll call you when I can." Then I'd hang up. Lucy was smart—she saved every number I ever called from, even if it was from a store, so she'd know it was me if I ever called again.

Sometimes, when things got bad, I'd walk to the store and pay to make two quick calls. I didn't know what else to do. Every time I managed to leave, I'd somehow end up back with him. He wouldn't leave me alone.

I even started writing notes with phone numbers and messages for people to pass along. When they came to buy weed, I'd slip them the note and beg, "Please don't open this now. If Maine Maine sees me talking to you, he'll beat me again. I can't go back to the hospital." A few people helped, but most didn't. Some threw the notes away as soon as they left.

One of the few people who actually came through was Vanquese, a guy Chase's dad used to run around with. I knew he liked me, so I used that to my advantage. I had him pull up to the house and told him to wait while I grabbed my things. I had everything packed, ready to go to Lucy's. I made it to his car, but just as I was about to leave, Maine Maine came outside.

He saw me and started yelling, "Where the fuck do you think you're going with my bitch? Where's her shit?" Vanquese didn't flinch.

He looked Maine Maine dead in the eye and said, "That's not your bitch, my dog. Amanda's leaving. She ain't staying here."

But it didn't end there. Maine Maine beat the shit out of Vanquese right in front of me. He hit him so hard, I found out later that Vanquese had to have his jaw wired shut from the damage. Then it was my turn. Maine Maine dragged me out of the car, hitting me again and again. I lost count after the sixth punch. I passed out at some point, and when I woke up, I was on the floor of that same apartment. I remember the feeling of hopelessness that morning. The mattress we had wasn't even on a proper frame—it was sitting on milk crates. I couldn't call

71

for help; no one could save me.

At times, he'd try to make it up to me, pretending things were normal. He'd suggest I go out with the other women in the complex to get my nails done, but even then, it felt like I was being monitored. The girls would gossip, report back to him, and act like nothing was wrong.

One day, we went to a nail shop on Elvis Presley Boulevard. As I sat there, the nail technician asked what I wanted. I couldn't even focus. I got up and went next door to Turtles to get a chicken and rice bowl. I sat on the curb and ate, trying to gather my strength. When I returned to the chair, I still didn't know what to say.

"I don't know," I finally told her. "When I'm ready, I'll let you know. Just give me a minute."

The women around me started whispering. "Girl, what's wrong with you?" they asked.

I wanted to scream, "Everything! You've seen it all for the past two years and haven't said a word!" But instead, I stayed quiet.

They told me, "Just get your nails done. It'll make you feel better." But nothing could make me feel better. Not there, not then.

Another time, I ended up in jail. I had been driving a red car, and when I was pulled over, I got arrested. While I was in the holding cell, this girl started talking about how she was "with her man." Lo and behold, her man was Maine Maine. She was locked up with me, one of the girls he had been cheating on me with.

Of course, I was furious. I felt so stupid for even caring about him, let alone fighting over him, but in that moment, I couldn't hold back. We got into a fight right there in the holding cell.

It got so bad that the guards separated us, putting me in a different holding cell by myself.

When I was moved to the back, I managed to get in touch with Lucy.

I told her, "Hey, I'm locked up." She already knew. "

I'm with your mom right now," she said. That threw me off. "You're with my mom?"

"Yeah," she said. "Your mom is trying to get your car back. Maine Maine won't answer her calls, and nobody's doing anything about it. Cry Baby, I know you and your mom don't always see eye to eye, but she's your mom, and I've got her back just like you've always had my mom's back."

Hearing that meant everything to me. "Thank you so much," I told her. "I know she's probably a nervous wreck."

"She is," Lucy replied. "But don't worry—I've got her. Your mom is my mom, and my mom is your mom. I don't care how messed up they are; they're still our parents."

While I was still locked up, my mom and Lucy decided to take matters into their own hands. Together, they hatched a plan to get my car back from Maine Maine.

In broad daylight, my mom and Lucy pulled up to Oakshire, where Maine Maine was holed up in a trap house. He was inside, blasting music, people coming and going, too distracted to notice anything happening outside. My mom played her role perfectly. She waited until the trap house was busy and chaotic so he wouldn't notice the car.

When the time was right, my mom pulled up, and Lucy jumped out, got into my car, and drove off. My mom followed right behind her. Lucy was ready for anything. She dared anyone to touch my mom or stop her. She had made up her mind that if anyone tried, she would shoot her way out of there.

Nobody was going to mess with them or take my car.

Maine Maine was planning to destroy my car so I'd have nothing when I got out of jail, but thanks to my mom and Lucy, he didn't get the chance. I know my mom and I don't have the best relationship, but at the end of the day, she's still my mom. I respect her for what she did that day. No matter our differences, she proved that when it really matters, she's in my corner.

7

Club Envy Brooks Road

By the time we moved to Hillview, I was seeing Chicago regularly. He knew I was with Maine Maine, but Chicago would pull up in a different car every time, so Maine Maine wouldn't know it was him. We had a system. I'd sneak out to meet him, and when I came back, I wouldn't get beat. Things started to get complicated when Maine Maine wanted to meet Chicago.

He said, "I'll get out and meet him. Tell him I can put you on some money."

Chicago got out of the car and walked in to meet Maine Maine. They started talking, and I got into the truck with Chicago.

He told me, "I'm going to take you to this strip club called Envy. You're gonna work there. I'll make your payout, pay me back, and after that, you'll be on your own."

I was nervous. I'd never worked at a strip club before and didn't even know if I could dance.

Chicago just said, "Tonight's your first night. Let's see how it goes." So, I went. The whole strip club scene started out kind of unexpectedly. Chicago suggested I go, and even offered to pay for my first night there. Maine Maine gave me the money for shoes, an outfit, and everything I needed to get started. I walked into the club without having to audition, simply because I knew the right people. Maine Maine and Chicago were there, and they handled everything. I thought that if I was around these guys, it would help me make money, but I had a lot to learn.

My first night wasn't great. I didn't know the routine, and the money was scarce, but I learned quickly. I had to pick a name for myself, which was tough at first. My initial choice, "Memphis," was already taken, but I settled on "Cry Baby," a nickname people had called me for always being emotional. The DJ didn't miss a beat when I gave him the name and asked me if I was sure about it. I was, and it stuck.

The first night, I didn't make much money, only about $180, and when I got home around 4 AM, Maine Maine was all about asking how much I made, questioning my spending, and hyping me up. I had to show him my shoes and outfit, and while I did give him a small amount of the money, I kept most of it hidden. I didn't trust him enough to be open about my earnings.

The second night went better. I learned more about how the club worked and how to approach people, but then things took a weird turn. I saw a neighbor from the apartment I'd lived in with Said before it burned down. Seeing him made me anxious, so I ran backstage to change and calm down. When I came back out for a drink, he approached me, and we exchanged some small talk. He asked if I had set the fire, and I joked back, "I don't know, did I?" It was an awkward conversation, but we laughed it off. Then, he offered me $300, saying it was to cover my payout for the night and told me to keep the rest. I wasn't fooled, though; I knew what was going on.

The third night at the strip club, I remember it as Fear's Day.

76

This is the night that I got kidnapped. A little backstory is that Maine Maine would leave me one a day to smoke and so he didn't know, but I would smoke with Amp. He would give me weed to smoke or I would pay him back later. We became cool and gained a friendship over it; basically, Maine Maine was doing me bad, so I gained friendships with people that would be lasting, where I would actually make money with later on. They knew I was very honest, loyal and straight up. I never steal. I don't do it; I won't. When that shit happened with my parents, I vowed to never ever do that shit again, and I never did because I saw, and I knew how bad it could fuck up a relationship.

So back to the third night in the strip club. This is the night where a party was brought in and there was probably about eight guys in one group, six in another, and four in another. The club was packed. We didn't have enough girls for all the guys that were in there that night. There were guys tugging on me asking for dances wanting this and that. I was doing really good. I made about $900.

A couple of guys asked me, "Do you wanna go back and do a party?"

I said, "No, I'm good. I gotta go ahead and do my payout. I'm out for the night. You know, my time's up." I would do whatever I could do just to get away from that group. They were very aggressive.

They argued, "Oh, we already paid your payout. So you going with us."

Again, I was like, "No, I'll give you the money. I'll pay you for what you pay for pay out. I'm not going with you."

And they're like, "No, it don't work like that."

Well, it just so happens that's the night that I was there by myself. I got dropped off by Maine Maine. There was also another guy. Ted, from Hillview. He's known; he's big in the drug game. People know him because he's a Vice Lord.

I was texting Amp the whole time, telling him I think something bad is about to happen. I'm about to get kidnapped.

He was like, "OK, just hold on, try to hold out as long as you can, you know, just hold out."

And so I was like, "OK, I'm, I'm trying. But they're persistent."

Security was dealing with another situation, so there was nobody by the dressing room door where we go in and change out and, you know. Put our shit in our bag or get ready or whatever. But group of guys were right by the door trying to get me to go with them. So I was thinking, I can't just stay here in this fucking room forever.

Amp called me and was like, "Hey, Ted's is outside. He's trying to get you through all this."

I asked, "Ted, who's he with?"

Amp said, "He just by himself, fuck me. Why he need to be with somebody?"

I said, "They're this is a group of guys and it's just me, little old white girl. They're gonna fucking tear me up, and there's no way just one guy is going to be able to get these guys up off of me."

He was like, "I'm telling you, Ted's outside waiting on you now."

I asked, "He can't come in?"

He said, "No, he's not fixing to pay to come in just to come and get you. Go outside!"

I said, "Oh my God, I'm so scared! Alright. If anything happens, you know this is what I'm wearing and I left at this time."

He said, "I got the phone call, I got what time you called me last." I said OK and walked outside the dressing room.

One guy had me by one arm. Another guy had already grabbed my stripper bag. There was one guy walking with the keys like to the car to get in the driver's side. When we came outside of the strip club doors, there was somebody parked right in the front.

Lo and behold, there was Ted and he hollered, "Hey, what you doing my fucking cuz like?!"

At this point I already knew what it was; you had to play your role. He don't give a fuck if I was a bitch or what?

And so he is like," Hey, dog, yo bitch. She didn't say she had a party."

That's when I caught on to what was going on; he was acting like he's pimping me out and I'm his bitch. Basically, I'm his property. They can't do shit with me until they pay him. Then they can do whatever.

And they're like, "Hey, dog, we just paid her pay out."

I was like, "No, I offered it back.

Ted said, "Shut the fuck up and get in the car!"

The guys were like, "Nah, hell Nah, you don't do shit!" They had me by the wrist, and I was looking at Ted.

The main guy asked, "Who is you?" "I'm Ted." he answered. "Ted's, who?" he replied. And he said "Ted from the Hillview Apartments. We do something like that in the VL."

One of the guys said, "Oh, fuck, let that bitch go. We don't want shit to do with that. Go and get your hoe."

Ted told me again, "Get in the fucking car." I got in the car and didn't say shit. Of course I played my role and when we got in the car, the other guys pulled off. He hadn't even put the keys in the ignition yet. He grabbed my arm and I kind of grabbed it back.

He's like, "No, you alright? I told him "No," and he was like "It's alright. I know that shit's kind of scary. I know I kind of shook you up a little bit back there, but I had to do that. It is crazy out here. You could have ended up dead. What the fuck do they got you doing in the strip club anyway?"

I said, "I don't know. I don't even know how to dance, so I don't know why they put me in here anyway."

He said, "Man, this shit ain't no good, so this isn't gonna end up happening to you. No, man, I'm gonna tell them this shit, this shit ain't no good. This shit ain't gonna fly over here. I'm gonna make sure this shit don't never happen."

I said that sounded good to me, but that shit don't just happen like that, and he ain't gonna make them stop.

He said," You ain't stripping no more in Memphis. I can tell you that much."

I don't know what happened, but when I got dropped off, Maine Maine told me to go in the house. Amp, Maine Maine, Hammer; everybody they stepped outside and had some type of talk and I never went to the strip club again.

I was still navigating through a lot of complicated situations at the time, mostly through relationships that offered financial benefits, as I needed the money to get by. Some of the people I met were just passing through town, like a lawyer I encountered one night. He was a regular at some of the upscale spots, and he made it clear that he wanted to spend time with me, but it wasn't about anything physical. Instead, he paid for the entire experience.

We would go out for fancy dinners, and he'd rent expensive outfits for me to wear, always at five-star venues. He never asked for anything in return besides my company, but there was one condition—he had a habit that required him to have access to certain substances. I would help him with that, making sure he had what he needed.

We had a very specific arrangement where I would meet him, and we'd enjoy the evening, but he would wait until the very end of the night to indulge. This way, I didn't have to be around during the aftermath, as I knew how difficult it could be when someone was coming down from a high. After the date, I would return everything I borrowed—clothes, jewelry, whatever it was—and he would give me my payment for the night. A car service would then take me home. It was a transaction that was almost like a business deal, but it helped me stay afloat for a time.

So then another time, there was this trick. I went out drinking and I was drinking at this bar called Celtic Crossing at Midtown. I met this guy; he was a trucker and he was just in town for the night because he was on a route. It was winter time, so it was really nasty, wet, and cold. It was a wet cold, not like a dry cold. We came up to a mutual agreement of $500.00 for an hour, and that would be in the hotel that he would get. After that hour he would leave the hotel, too, so that ensured me a place to stay for the night and the money to have the next day. Basically I had just secured myself for the next few days through this one. Once again, very transactional. This guy was the weirdest guy I think I had ever dealt with. He stopped and got condoms.

Of course, nothing would ever happen without a condom, but when we got to the room he was like, "I don't want you. I don't want to do you. I want you to do me."

And I was like. "Well, OK, so you like, you want me to get on top? You want me to like, basically take control of my head is what you were thinking."

81

CRY BABY, DON'T CRY

And he was like, "I want you to turn me around and put it in me" In my head. I was thinking I don't have anything to put in you.

That was what I was thinking in my head, but my response out loud was, "I've never done this before. Baby, you'll have to teach me. I'm new."

And he said, "Oh, that turns me on even more."

I quickly learned that he wanted me to fist him in his ass. And how I would do this is stick my hand into the condom, and at first I do one finger, then two fingers, then three fingers. After I get to three fingers, I then take my fingers out. I put all of them together. All of my fingers together and I slide my hand into the hole. And fist them and I go back and forth as slow or fast as they want it to go. And that's what I call *fucking a male." That was my first time ever doing that. After he left, I threw up and took about 12 showers. That was so fucking nasty.

That night, I had called someone I knew, Chicago, asking for help. I told him that I had a hotel room but didn't have any money—though I actually did, I just needed to save it for the next few days. He responded by bringing over some food, and though he had to leave quickly, he assured me that if I needed anything, he would help. It wasn't about money or anything else—he was there when I needed him, and that's what mattered to me. It was so different from what I had experienced before. Most people didn't want to help or would make me feel bad for needing it. But this was different.

I felt a sense of unconditional support from him, something I hadn't often encountered. The only other people who had shown me this kind of care were Lucy, her family, and Chicago. That's why I felt so deeply connected to them—it was a bond of genuine care and love.

Later, I had an encounter with someone who tried to take advantage of me. We had met earlier, and it was clear from his behavior that he intended to manipulate the situation for his own benefit. He made assumptions about me and the situation, thinking I would just comply. When we got to the hotel room, he said he needed a shower first, but his attitude suggested that he was expecting more than just a simple interaction. I made it clear that I wasn't there for what he thought. I didn't feel right about it, so I trusted my instincts and left the situation. I called a friend, and they came to pick me up. It wasn't the first time I had to trust my gut, but it was one of the most important moments where I realized that leaving was the best choice.

8

Chicago

I never told Maine Maine about that night, or really about a lot of things. We all knew how he'd react, and when he reacted, that's when things would go downhill for me—something would be broken, bruised, or hurt. So, that night, we went to the casino. When I first saw him, Chicago, I was immediately attracted to him—physically and mentally. I didn't know him yet, but there was something about him. He was so smooth, so grown, so secure. He was older, had his life together, and actually worked—unlike the jobs I was used to seeing. He had real money.

When we got to the casino, he asked for my number. He said he had a couple of people who could help me make money. I knew exactly what he meant. He had people who were interested in me, and I needed to get his number if I wanted to get involved. If I wanted any money, I had to play the game and be real slick about it, but I couldn't let anyone know. Lucy's family was the only real family I had, and they wouldn't approve of any of this, so, I had to be careful.

Once I got his number, I won't lie, things started moving fast.

He gave me the numbers of a couple of his friends. We went out a few times, but whenever I was around them, they'd ask how much. Then, they'd give me the money and go off to the room, but when we got in the car, he'd tell me, "Shorty, get in the car." When we went to the room, he wouldn't let them do anything. Instead, he'd pay me and have sex with me himself. It made me think—did he actually want me? Did he love me? Or was he just helping me out? Why was he doing this for me? Why was I different from all the other women he could have?

I was younger, had nothing to offer, and came from a broken home. I was messed up, bruised, and struggling. So why me? But with Terry, we kept it all quiet. Maine Maine never knew about him, but everyone else knew about us. The thing with Chicago was, nobody knew him. I kept him a secret. It was like a piece of candy nobody else could have, and if I wanted it, I had to save it for when I really needed or wanted something. That's when I'd call him. That's when he'd show up. It was like having my own hood Superman from Chicago, wearing jeans, a white T-shirt, and Timberlands—he wasn't afraid of anything. He drove a dually truck, and he had this heavy-duty gun with a drum magazine plus a 32 extended clip. He never missed a shot. His name held weight in the streets—he was respected. It was all so different from what I was used to, and honestly, it was kind of relaxing.

Sometimes, when we'd have our little meetups and have sex, I'd think, I don't want him to leave, but as soon as we were done, he had to go. He'd leave me at the hotel so I could relax and not go back to Maine Maine's place for the night. I'd make up some excuse, like staying with Lucy or something else that might fly under the radar. It didn't really matter because he knew he was also cheating, so it gave him his own time to do

85

whatever he wanted, too.

I was living with Maine Maine, messing around with Terry, and talking to Chicago. And Chicago, he brought me a couple of people who'd pay for everything. If I went out with anyone, they'd pay for my drinks, my food—anything I needed. I didn't even pay for my own stuff half the time, and if someone I just met came along, they'd pay for their share, too. People around me knew what was up. I'd be at a bar off Madison like Boscos, Bayou, Babalu, Blue Monkey, etc. Sometimes I'd see my sister, and think, oh great, she's gonna catch me with my sugar daddy. She'd see me getting taken out to dinner or being given money, and she'd know what was really going on.

Sometimes I'd look at her, and she'd look back and just know. I'd walk over to her, saying, "This isn't what I think." I wasn't with sugar daddies just for the money. Yeah, I'd get money from them, but I wasn't sleeping with them all the time. After the first time, I didn't have to do it again. They just wanted someone to share their life with—someone to go out to dinner with, to drink and party with. They were living the life they never had because they worked too hard to have it before. They were using me to live that life.

When I say tricks, I mean I'd meet guys, do my thing, and get paid—maybe $250 for an hour. Once that was done, I'd leave and never talk to them again. But with the sugar daddies, it was different. They were regulars. I ended up with three, and yeah, some of them were older, but that was just a bonus.

In relationships, especially with someone like Maine Maine, business and personal life never mix well. I can't make money together in a healthy way. I had learned that lesson the hard way, so I knew I couldn't work with him. I needed a way to handle the situation, so I reached out to Chicago, for help. He had always been there for me before, and I knew he could help again. I told him I needed clients and some help getting things started.

Chicago came through, helping me get the clients I needed. But he made it clear that he wasn't going to let me have sex with them—he'd handle that part, and I'd get the money they would've paid me. I told him I didn't want to do that, and he respected my decision, stopping that arrangement. He even tried to suggest I work at a strip club, but I turned that down too. I wasn't willing to sell my body anymore. I just wanted to make money selling drugs, like I had been selling weed before.

He didn't judge me. He never made me feel less than. He treated me like an equal. Around him and Lucy's family, I felt like I wasn't defined by what I'd done or what I was going through. He treated me with dignity, always trying to help me get back on my feet, and to see the potential in myself when I couldn't.

By now, I wasn't with Maine Maine anymore, but I was still in contact with him. I was living with Lucy but still going back to Hillview, talking to him and doing my own thing. I'd gotten Maine Maine completely out of my life, but I still kept an eye on him, partly because I wanted him to feel the pain and jealousy I had felt. I wanted him to understand what I'd been through.

At first I was also talking to Amp at this point. There was a bond between us—a kind of unspoken love. We didn't say it out loud, but we both knew we could count on each other, no matter what. We were there for each other through the mess, trying to make it out together.

I was starting to work with Amp, who already knew every-thing. When I told him I had heroin, he didn't need me to explain the details—he already knew the numbers, the street value, and who the players were. He was connected in his neighborhood, and I was the outsider trying to find my way. At this point, I had to observe, listen, and learn how things worked around here.

I didn't call it "recruiting," but I ended up teaming up with a few people. I teamed up with Amp, Dello, and a guy I knew through Dello, whose sister was Nee Poo. Dello was her boyfriend, so he reported to Amp. He also had two uncles—Icky and Rat Tat. They were well-known, and Rat Tat got his name from the sound of his gunshots, which were loud and fast, like the rhythm of "rat-tat."

Now, I had these people working with me. But the issue was, nobody was reporting directly to me, and that's when things got complicated. Amp already had the dope, and everyone knew Maine Maine was out of the picture. Even Hammer came to Amp asking where it was coming from. So, I made a plan: I'd drop off the heroin—about 10 grams at a time, sometimes a little more—just the basics for now.

I told Amp, "I handle this. I give your guys what they need, and they report back to I. I'm not dealing with anyone else. My name stays off of everything."

Amp agreed, but he made it clear that everyone already knew I had it. The important part was, if anyone wanted to get to me, they had to go through him. He made that message clear to everyone in Hillview. If something happened to me, Amp would handle it. If he couldn't, he had other people, like March and Hammer, who would back him up.

At this point, I had the respect I needed. People knew I was serious, and I had protection. I carried a gun for safety, but I never had to use it because I knew others would take care of that for me. It was all about keeping control, making sure I stayed untouchable, and building the kind of reputation that would keep me safe.

I was pulling up to Hillview, staying sharp, checking the scene, picking up money, and dropping off dope. This routine went on for a while. During that time, I noticed Maine Maine with his truck, trying to get it running. He was always struggling with it, but after a while, I saw him driving it for a couple of days straight. That's when I realized he finally had it running.

I wasn't worried about it, but I knew I had to stay ahead. I called Nipu—Amp's sister. She was cool with me, and her boyfriend, Dello, was making money off my dope. That gave me some leverage, knowing that whatever I said would have weight. So, I called her up one night and told her I was coming over. We were pretty close at that point; we'd even gone Christmas shopping together for our families.

I wasn't planning on staying in one spot too long, though. If you hang out too much in a place where you're dealing with money, it makes people envious, and eventually, they'll try to take you out. That's just the way things went when people weren't making money with you. So, I always made sure to keep moving, maybe spending 30 minutes to an hour before I bounced, sometimes even leaving for hours before coming back.

One night, I called up Nee Poo and told her I was coming over. She was getting off work later, and I said I'd be there to hang out and smoke. Nothing serious, just wanted to peep some things. She agreed and told me to pull up. When I got there, we went inside, and I could see Maine Maine through the window across the parking lot. He was getting ready to call it a night, shaking hands with someone and telling them to go ahead and

89

lay down. I knew exactly what that meant—he was done for the night, and I could take my shot.

I needed to make a quick run to the Hillview store. It was a small spot, more of a convenience store than anything else, but Amir, who owned it, and I had become familiar through other hustles. I grabbed some chocolate and candy bars—enough to make sure I could mess with Maine Maine's truck. I had Rat Tat run it over to the truck and stuff it all in the gas tank. I wanted to see it fail without anyone knowing I was behind it. He came back, and I gave him some dope to get high for doing it.

But as luck would have it, Maine Maine drove the truck around again, and it was still running fine. I couldn't believe it. There's no way candy bars and M&Ms wouldn't mess it up. I thought to myself, "This isn't working," so I made another call.

I told Nee Poo, "I need some Similac—the baby formula."

She was confused at first. "For what?" she asked.

I explained, "Just a little bit. I'm going to put it in his gas tank. It'll absorb the gas and keep the truck from cranking." She thought I was crazy, but she went along with it.

Once I got the formula, I headed to the truck and poured it into the tank. I didn't stop there—I keyed his truck too. I wrote my name on the side so he'd know exactly who did it. It was a message. Now, he couldn't touch me. I had the power because he couldn't retaliate. He knew that, and that's why I could do what I wanted without fear.

The next morning, around 4 or 5 AM, I woke up and went outside. Sure enough, Maine Maine was out there, livid. His truck was dead, and he was cursing up a storm, calling me all kinds of names. I stood back and watched him lose it.

I didn't let him see me. I had parked my car in a spot where he couldn't trace it back to me. My Honda Civic, which I had gotten from my sister after she upgraded, was parked far enough out of sight. I'd been careful not to leave any clues. I wasn't about to make it easy for him. I went back to Lucy's place to fill her in on what happened, and I kept a low profile for the rest of the day. All in all, that was another chapter in the chaos of Hillview—things were always tense, always on the edge.

Things were good for a while. I was living at Lucy's house, still seeing my Maine Maine every now and then, but nothing serious between us anymore. At this point, I'd gotten super close with Lucy's nephew. Everybody knew what it was, but no one said anything—just one of those unspoken things. Even when he messed with other girls, it was whatever. We didn't talk about it, but we knew.

Now, Lucy had this guy she was talking to named <u>Yo</u>. He was a big deal—money stacked on top of money, houses, gold chains, all that flashy stuff. We'd hang out with different guys, go to their houses, smoke, and do our thing. I remember one night, Yo invited us over to his place to kick back.

He was all like, "Come through, let's smoke and chill," but Lucy was on him about the gas money. She'd just met him, and he hadn't given her anything yet, so she wasn't about to go anywhere with him without that.

He said, "I got you," real smooth, like he'd do whatever she wanted. This guy was whipped, no question. To him, Lucy was Cleopatra, and he'd do anything to please her. It was crazy to see how far he'd go for her.

So, we all went to his house—me, Lucy, and her cousin. We never did things alone; we always stuck together. If something went down, at least one of us could be the backup, I know? We'd be the ones to tell what happened, make sure everyone was safe.

We always had each other's backs.

We weren't just three girls rolling around either—trust, we had other things going on with other guys. But no matter what, we never went anywhere without each other. Over time, me and Lucy got even closer. We were like sisters at this point. Braiding our hair on the same porch, laughing, living life, having fun. It was a good time, the kind of time that made I forget about the rest of the world.

One time when we went with Yo, we followed him back to his house, and once we got there, he started playing music and trying to set the vibe. But we were like, "We're ready to go," and he said, "Hold up, I'll make it worth your time. I'll give you some money." Next thing I know, he started throwing cash up in the air.

My cousin turned around and said, "I hope I don't think this means we're shaking anything, but I sure as hell am picking up this money." She started grabbing it, and I just followed her lead, staying quiet because, well, I know, the white girl always says something offbeat, and it's better not to get involved. So there I was, picking up the cash.

Yo was cool with it. He just said, "I just wanna see your friend." Lucy wasn't having it though.

She was like, "Maybe another time." He had a friend with him who was acting super weird. He had to be on something. Definitely wasn't just drunk—it had to be coke or something.

He kept going on about how good the white girl looked. "I don't wanna talk to you, Lucy, I wanna talk to the white girl," he kept saying.

We just laughed it off and said, "Yeah, we're about to go," trying to wrap things up.

But Yo wouldn't let up, kept asking Lucy, "Where you going?

Where you going?" I was heading for the door, but as I walked, his friend dropped to his knees, begging me not to leave. "Please, don't go. You're so fine, You're so beautiful."

I told him, "We gotta go," trying to push past him.

I had one leg at the door when this guy grabbed my leg with both hands, pulling me back in. Then he grabbed my face with his hands and kissed me on the cheek. I had his teeth marks on me for weeks after that.

I was freaked out and said, "He's nuts, I need a rabies shot." Lucy and her cousin just started laughing, but I knew it was time to leave, so I got us out to the car.

Even then, he wouldn't stop. He followed us all the way to the car, asking what it'd take to keep us there.

"I'll give you a ride home," he said.

Lucy said, "Hell no, we came together, we're leaving together." Then she hit him with, "But it'd be nice to get something to eat on the way home," and that's when he pulled out another $200 or $300, just trying to smooth-talk his way into keeping us around.

But Lucy wasn't new to this. She wasn't some rookie. Her brothers and nephews had taught her the ropes. She was all woman—graceful, feminine—but if you pushed her too far, she could fight and throw down like any guy. I never wanted to mess with her like that.

One time, I remember us all going to the club. There used to be this strip club called Platinum Plus, and it eventually shut down. Platinum Plus was where my dad and my uncle Angel used to hang out, having drinks and doing their thing. When we were little, I'd see it all the time—shut down for various reasons, people making coke deals and other shady stuff. I'm sure Angel had something to do with it, especially with all the connections he had. My dad eventually stopped going because it just wasn't worth the trouble, and he didn't want to risk anything happening and getting caught up in something that could hurt us.

After Platinum Plus shut down, another club took its place for a while, but I can't quite remember the name of it. It was right in front of Piccadilly off Mount Moriah. Terry's birthday is May 11th, and mine is May 9th, so we always had that one-day gap between our birthdays. We'd celebrate mine on the 9th, take a little break on the 10th, and then go all out for Terry's on the 11th.

One year, we decided, "Let's just go out. We're sick of this." Terry had some homeboys who could get us into the club, and we just wanted to celebrate. He wanted to celebrate his birthday, and I wanted to celebrate mine. I had just bought myself a nice watch, a real piece of jewelry, and it felt like the perfect time to go out. So, we hit the club, and we had an amazing time. We were all dancing, drinking, just having a blast. Lucy was having a great time, I was too, and Terry was enjoying himself. It was one of those nights I wish I could relive because it was honestly one of the best memories I have.

Another memory with Lucy was when she had a friend named Alicia. Alicia hated me, and I think it was because I became Lucy's best friend. Before me, Lucy and Alicia were inseparable, but once I came around, it was like we became unbreakable— sisters in every sense. Nothing could tear us apart, and still, no one can come between us. If anyone tried to say anything about the other, we already knew what was up.

Alicia started acting differently once I was in the picture. She'd get funny with me, and come to find out, it was because she was jealous of the bond Lucy and I had. I never understood

94

it. How can you be jealous of your best friend? You should be supporting them, cheering them on, not trying to compete with them. But that's exactly what Alicia did. Whatever Lucy did, Alicia tried to do right after her—sometimes even trying to outdo her. If Lucy got a car, Alicia would get the same one, just a different color. If Lucy had a baby, Alicia would have one, too. It was almost like she was obsessed with her, and I never really understood why.

I remember this one time when Alicia had just gotten an apartment and was having a party. She had a pole set up and some dancers came in to perform. Terry was driving his T-top Thunderbird, and Lucy was in her silver Cadillac. When we arrived at the party, Terry and I couldn't keep our hands off each other. We were always like that, always joking and having fun. We could never stay mad at each other for too long. If we fought, it was never serious.

We'd end up laughing it off, asking, "Where you at?" and, "I miss you." So when we got there, we didn't even bother going to the party. We just went straight to the backseat and started... well, you know.

Once we finished, we looked up and saw that everyone else had already gone inside.

Lucy was like, "Where the hell are Terry and Cry Baby?" So she came outside, and when she saw me getting out of the passenger seat, adjusting my dress, she was like, "Oh damn!" Terry, all flustered, was like, "My bad, TT, I'm coming!" He was trying to pull up his pants, and we both scrambled to straighten ourselves out before heading into the party. But honestly, the party wasn't that great. It was pretty lame, so we all decided to leave. We ended up at Lucy's place, smoked, drank, and just made it our own little session.

Another time, Terry and I were messing around pretty heavily. I ended up pregnant by him, and of course, Lucy was the first to know. But at the same time, Terry was talking to another girl, Molly. This girl lived just down the street from Lucy's house on Hallowell. I told Lucy, and at that point, Terry and I weren't really talking, trying to get over each other. We decided to move on and talk to other people. But since I was pregnant, it changed everything. I wasn't about to just let it go. I told Terry, "We're not moving on, we need to figure this out."

So, Lucy and I decided to get a little petty. We went to Terry's car and stuck pregnancy tests and pads all over it. We didn't tell him it was us, but we knew. He was confused, to say the least, but we never admitted it. I ended up losing the pregnancy and going through an abortion, which was a lot to handle on top of everything else going on.

9

Chosen Family

Over time, I began to notice patterns in how some people treated me—especially in situations where power dynamics were at play. There were moments where I was made to feel small, like my worth was only tied to how others saw me or what they wanted. I wasn't always treated with respect, but I learned to navigate these situations. I realized that sometimes the best way to handle things was to stand my ground and not let anyone dictate how I should feel or behave. It's a lesson that has stayed with me.

In Memphis, BBQ is king. We have the International Barbecue Cooking Contest in May-every year. Throughout the city you will hear people giving advice about the best tricks of the trade, who has the best sauce and sides. There are BBQ shops all over the city. There are the famous restaurants that have won awards and are featured on various tv shows like Corky's, The Rendezvous, The BBQ Shop, Central BBQ, and Payne's Bar-B-Que. There are almost as may ways to spell BBQ than there are sauces. These are just some of the big names. There are mom and pop shops all over the city. Corner stores and even grills in front yards selling a plate. One thing that they all share is that BBQ goes hand in hand with hospitality. It is kindness and neighborliness at the heart of it all. Cooking and laughing together, regardless of race, class, and other things that divide us, BBQ brings people together, and it is deep felt generosity that led Mama May and Papa Lee to take me in and care for me. They were the owners of Pollard's BBQ, which is now call A&R BBQ.

When we were at Mama May and Papa Lee's house, and it was always the same routine. He would get up first, turn on the TV, and that's how we knew it was time to start waking up. When the TV clicked on, I knew it was safe to wander into the den and find him drinking his coffee, waking up slowly. Then she would get up, then Lucy. That's how it went, every day. When it was summer, it was the same, but when it came time for the kids to go to school, Papa Lee would be up early, and the whole house would be awake for the baby, Michael. Michael was the first grandchild, the first everything, and he was the center of everyone's world. He meant everything to everyone, and we all worked around his schedule.

Growing up, seeing the way my chosen parents interacted and supported each other shaped how I viewed relationships and love. Their marriage was the kind I always hoped to have one day—a partnership where both people were equal, where I could count on each other no matter what. There was never any doubt in my mind about the strength of their bond, even when things weren't perfect. They taught me the importance of compromise, communication, and unconditional love. Even when they had their disagreements, they always seemed to find their way back to each other, and that was something that stuck with me.

When I was living at Lucy's house, there were times I needed a break, so I would randomly rent a hotel room for a day or two. It wasn't just for me—it was also to give her family a break from me, too. Living with someone can be challenging, even when I care for them, and I wanted to respect that. So, I would spend some time on my own, and then go back to her house.

During those times, if I was seeing someone or dating, I would meet up with them at the hotel, but I never brought anyone back to Lucy's house. I never wanted to disrespect her family by bringing men over or making them uncomfortable. I valued the trust they gave me by letting me stay there, and I never wanted to take advantage of that.

I remember one time when I was with Lucy and Terry, we were running errands. I had just gotten a pack of pills that I planned to sell to make some money. As we were driving, I had the pills with me when we got pulled over by the police. In a panic, I swallowed the entire pack with some water from a cup that had been used for cigarettes and ash. Thankfully, the police let us go, and I rushed back to Lucy's house to tell her dad what happened. He insisted I make myself throw up to get rid of the pills. After a lot of effort, I was able to get them out, and it was like nothing ever happened. It wasn't ideal, but I was grateful that her family had my back at that moment.

Lucy, Terry, and I were like a team. It felt like we were the three amigos, and no matter what happened, I knew I could count on them. Lucy's brother, Lee Jr. , was always very private, sticking to himself and selling weed from the back room of the house. He had a way of keeping his life separate from ours, but he was always around, doing his own thing.

There were some tough times, like when one of Lee Jr. 's girlfriends went missing, and no one ever found out what happened to her. That still sticks with me, even though it was years ago. Despite these challenges, I always felt that Lucy's family welcomed me, especially during the holidays.

Christmas was a big deal with them. I remember how generous they were, especially when I couldn't afford gifts for my son, Chase. Mama May and Papa Lee would make sure they bought presents for him when they went shopping, and they did it without me asking. My family didn't know the truth behind the gifts—they thought it came from me—but I was always grateful for their support.

One year, I had a big argument with my parents right before Christmas. They didn't want me around, and it hurt. But I still made sure to buy gifts for Chase, thanks to Lucy's family. On Christmas Eve, my car broke down with all the gifts in the back seat, and I didn't know what to do. I was upset and didn't know who else to call. Thankfully, Lucy came to my rescue. She picked me up, and we made sure the gifts got to her parents' house, where they were waiting for Chase.

There were other times when I just wished I could go back to my own home, the way Lucy had her own life with her parents. I often wished for that kind of peace, but I knew that was never going to be my reality. Still, I held on to the hope that things could one day be different, even though I wasn't sure how or when that might happen.

I remember one time, Lucy and I were in her room, and I let her text my mom for me.

She said, "You just don't know how to talk to her. Let me handle it."

I agreed, and we went back and forth with the texts. I was reading them as they went, and everything seemed fine at first. Then Lucy read a message from my mom after she asked, "Can

I just park my car in your driveway? I'll sleep in it if I have to; I just need somewhere warm and safe."

Lucy knew that wasn't true—she knew I was staying at her parents' house and was fine. But she wanted to see how my mom would respond, to see if the things I'd told her were really true. At that point, Lucy didn't fully understand the extent of the issues between me and my mom. She'd heard my side of the story, but hearing the reality for herself was different. When she saw my mom's response telling me not to park my car at her house or she'd call the police, Lucy was shocked.

She looked at me and said, "I don't know what's wrong with your mom."

I said, "I know, I've messed up in the past, but it's just the way things are now. I don't think it'll ever be different."

After that, I just gave up trying to fix things. I knew I was wrong, but there was nothing I could do to change it. The mother-daughter relationship I had hoped for, the one I see in movies or read about in books, would never exist for us. It had always felt transactional with my mom, and I never felt like she did things out of love. It was more like she did them out of guilt because she couldn't give me the relationship I needed. If I'd had that love, maybe things would've been different. But without it, I learned to survive on my own, even if that meant sleeping in the park. I've done that before—slept in the park overnight, only to wake up the next day and call Lucy for help.

She'd always come through, saying, "Girl, why didn't you just come home?" And I'd feel bad, knowing how much they cared, even though I hated having to ask for help all the time. She'd say, "You're my sister. you're family. Don't worry about it, but if this happens again, I'm telling Mom and Dad. And we all know what that means." That was always love on their end.

No matter what we had—or didn't have—Mama May and Papa Lee made sure we always had enough. There were always good vibes, music in the background, and food on the grill. We'd all laugh, drink, and enjoy each other's company without anyone judging. I never had to worry about anyone criticizing me. They knew how to have fun, and they always made me feel like I belonged. Holidays weren't about what we didn't have but about being together, and there was always love, no matter what.

Then, there were the little things—like when I didn't have clothes to wear because I'd lost everything. I couldn't go out because I didn't have anything to wear, and Mama May always came to the rescue. She had clothes for every occasion, and I could always find something to wear in her closet. She would help me get dressed, tell me what looked good, and make sure I was ready to go. Mama May always knew how to make me feel good about myself. She and Daddy shared such a strong, unconditional love. No matter how tough things got, they always had each other's backs.

That's what I loved about them. No matter how bad things got, no matter how mad or sad they were, they never stopped being there for one another. Their love was unbreakable, and I could see that no matter how hard things got, they would always have each other. And that was something I always admired.

10

Bankruptcy Lawyer

By this point, I was back at Mom and Dad's, and things were hard. I didn't have a plan, didn't have anything stable. I was living off sugar daddies and spending the money as I got it, but I knew it wouldn't last forever. I knew I needed to figure out how to get my own place. Eventually, I went back to Mckellar Woods, though it is now called Highland Meadows; this is where I had previously burned down my apartment. But I ran into a problem: I couldn't get the utilities on. I was told I'd have to file bankruptcy because of how high my bills were. That's when I met Michael. He was supposed to help me with the bankruptcy, but once I met him, nothing was ever the same.

Michael was a man with a lot of power. He could make things happen in Memphis and Mississippi, and he wasn't shy about it. He made me think it was my fault for the situation I was in, and I knew deep down it wasn't. He asked me about my life, about Chase, and how I was handling everything on my own. When he found out I was a single mom, he asked if I'd want to go out with him sometime. I knew exactly what he was after, and at his age, I could see right through him. He wasn't fooling me.

He would invite me to his office, pay me $200, and we'd have drinks. But after an hour, it would always escalate. He didn't want to have regular sex; he liked to watch. It was disturbing, to say the least. But sometimes I felt trapped, like I had no other option. He'd keep me coming back for that money, and he knew I needed it. Chase would go into the break room to play, and Jimmy would watch me from the cameras in his office while I kept an eye on my son. We'd drink, and I'd find myself drinking what he drank—Maker's Mark whiskey. It hit me differently than anything else I'd ever drunk. Smooth going down, but once it hit, it was like a high that wouldn't end, and I couldn't stop.

I tried to lie to Michael, telling him I was going to nursing school to make him think I wasn't just depending on him. But the truth was, I didn't have a car and had to rely on other people to get to him. He grew tired of it, so he promised to help me. He told me he would buy me a car, and he had me pick one out—a gold Camry. I was still juggling Terry and Maine Maine, but I didn't have any man living with me. I finally had a place of my own where I didn't have to walk on eggshells. I had control, and for the first time, it felt like my own safe space.

I knew where this was heading, so I made sure to cover myself. I printed out a few pictures of me, just in case anything happened to Michael or he tried something. In the world I was in, the "sugar daddy" and "trick" world, it was common to keep tabs on each other, to stay informed about what was happening on the street. At that time, I'd heard stories of girls getting involved with lawyers and then disappearing to avoid any exposure. I couldn't be sure if Michael would do the same to me, so I took precautions.

I planted pictures of myself in his office—random books on the shelves, his study area—pictures of me in lingerie and other more intimate photos. The reason I did this was simple: if anything ever happened to me, if I went missing or anything dark went down, I wanted the world to know who I was. I wanted the people who came after me to find the evidence. I wasn't going to let them paint me as someone I wasn't— someone they could dismiss or erase from the story.

I figured if anything came out, if his wife ever found out or if something worse happened to me, at least there would be some trace of who I was. The pictures would be a link to me, and they would show who I was to him. It would tie him to me, and if I went missing, I wasn't going to leave them with nothing. I wasn't going to let my son grow up with no answers, no closure. I had watched enough true crime shows—*Dateline*, *The First 48*—to know how these things can go, how easy it is for someone to just disappear, and I couldn't risk it. I wanted to make sure that if something happened to me, there would be something—anything—that could lead them back to the truth.

Michael was nice, and he was cool in his own way. He tried to give me experiences that he thought I'd never had, like taking me to the Horseshoe Casino. He'd get a room for us to spend the night, sometimes for two nights, but he'd always leave before the night was over, leaving the room for me to keep. It was a strange arrangement. He'd take me there, and either I'd ride back with him or stay on my own. Sometimes I'd invite friends to the room or just enjoy the space by myself. He'd let me order room service and do things like that, trying to impress me, I guess, or maybe win me over in his own way.

There was one time he took me to his condo in Oxford. I knew it was his family's place because his wife's things were everywhere—family photos, personal items. It was just so strange. I had been involved with him for two years by then, and we had been meeting up at this apartment regularly, but something felt off. The trip to Oxford felt like a tipping point, like things were starting to unravel between us.

My relationship with Michael lasted about two years. It ended when things took a turn after some troubling incidents. It started with me trying to keep things casual. I had just bought a new TV for my apartment in Highland Meadows and asked him to come help me set it up, trying to maintain a friendly relationship. But I guess trying to stay on good terms wasn't possible.

I saw Michael again, and he told me that he had an STD. I wasn't worried about it because I had been tested regularly and was confident that I was fine. It felt like he was just trying to use this as an excuse to stop dealing with me. He had been pulling away for a while, and I could tell that the dynamic had changed. The effort wasn't the same anymore, and I didn't make him a priority after his unsettling fantasies, which made me lose interest.

Eventually, we stopped seeing each other. I would call him from time to time, asking for money when I really needed it, and it was always for things I wasn't sure how I'd manage without. But after a while, he told me to stop calling, and I realized I was on my own. While I still had the income coming in from heroin, it wasn't enough to keep things going. I was in a rough spot, still involved.

11

Spottswood

Things with me and Maine Maine weren't going well, so I moved out and returned to work; this time at Olive Garden. While I was working there, I met this girl—her name was Taylor—and she was staying with a guy named Felipe. Felipe lived in a place called Spottswood, so I started hanging out over there with them. Felipe was into drugs, and I knew he liked me, but I didn't like him in that way. He liked both guys and girls, but I wasn't into him like that. I knew that if I acted like I did, though, he might help me with stuff I needed, like getting out of a tough situation. It was like everything was transactional at this point. I could get some security for me and Maine Maine if things got really bad, like if we got kicked out.

I spent a few days at their place smoking weed and getting to know Felipe and his roommates, Chelsea and Taylor. Chelsea and Felipe did coke, while Taylor and I mostly stuck to weed. Eventually, Chelsea got a girlfriend and moved out, and a room opened up. At that point, Maine Maine and I were about to get kicked out of Kingsgate, since KC had left and we couldn't keep up with the bills. So, I went to Felipe and asked if we could rent one of the rooms. He said yes, and it worked out because Taylor was planning to leave too.

So, Felipe ended up moving into one of the rooms, and Maine Maine and I moved into another. Felipe didn't mind helping me, but he wouldn't do much for Maine Maine. He was still cheating on me during all of this, but now he had nowhere else to go, and he was leaning on me. I had stopped dealing heroin for a while, but things were still messy.

At this point, I had taken a break from selling heroin. I couldn't get in touch with Chicago, the guy I'd been working with. He always had a job and would keep in touch sporadically, which made things inconsistent. I quickly realized that dealing drugs through him wasn't reliable—it was always on his time, and I could never keep consistent clientele. So, I stopped working with him on that front, only dealing with smaller things like weed when necessary. I already made up my mind that I wasn't going to sell for him anymore; it just wasn't steady enough.

Instead, I was working at Olive Garden and driving Felipe's car to get to work. Maine Maine, on the other hand, was still selling drugs and chilling at Felipe's place. I had a warrant out for possession of marijuana or something related, which eventually landed me in jail for about a month or two. While I was locked up, they had a screen in DeSoto County jail where I could text message people. I texted Maine Maine, but he wouldn't respond or pick up the phone, of course. Felipe, though, was texting me everyday, asking how I was doing and counting down the days until I'd be out.

Felipe was checking in on me, offering support, and telling me he was looking forward to getting me food when I got out— everything that Maine Maine should have been doing. But when it came down to getting me out of jail, Felipe was the one who bailed me out. Maine Maine didn't. Felipe had to sell one of his extra cars and break it down for parts to come up with the bond money to get me out, which took about fourteen days.

When Felipe finally bailed me out, we went to the Waffle House in Hernando, right by the jail. He said, "I have to tell you something, but when I tell you, I won't believe me." At that moment, I was just hoping it wasn't that Maine Maine had stolen something from Felipe, and that he was kicking us out. I had my things packed, just in case, but I hoped it wasn't that bad.

Felipe eventually sat me down and told me the truth: "Maine Maine's been cheating on you, and he's been doing it in my house. I'm not okay with it." He explained that he didn't know how to confront Maine Maine about it, especially because of his volatile attitude when he was coming down from drugs. Felipe also made it clear that he wasn't happy about helping me while Maine Maine was cheating on me and causing issues. I respected Felipe for being honest with me.

One thing about Felipe is that I never betrayed him. If I respected someone and they respected me, I was always straight with them. I was upfront and honest about things. But if the relationship was transactional, and I felt like I was being used or lied to, then all bets were off. And in this case, it felt like things were getting out of control.

Felipe then showed me the video—proof of Maine Maine cheating with this girl in my house. She had been in the den, my room, the kitchen—multiple times. And she even knew I was in jail, asking when I'd be getting out, because she knew once I returned, she wouldn't be able to see Maine Maine anymore. She even mentioned how her friend, Sarah, was trying to get with him, too. By the time I got out of jail, I knew everything. Felipe had already clued me in, but I couldn't say anything, or we'd fight. So I stayed quiet and played my role.

Sarah started showing up at the house while I was out, acting like I didn't know what was going on. Felipe would tell me he was going to buy coke from her, but I knew it wasn't just business—he was also sleeping with her. One day, I had enough. I waited until Felipe left and then went straight to Sarah's apartment. I knocked on the door, and she answered, acting casual.

I shoved my way inside and told her, "I don't know what y'all have going on, but messing with my man in my house is not okay. And I swear, I'll hurt you if I keep this up." She tried to downplay it, but I wasn't having it. I said, "Don't lie to me, I know what I've been doing." That's when she admitted that she didn't trust the guy she was dealing with, and she was just hoping Felipe would give her free drugs.

I made it clear: "If I need dope, find someone else. Felipe's not your plug anymore." After that, she never came around again. Maine Maine later asked me why she wasn't answering his calls or texting him back. He noticed she wasn't getting any more dope from him. I just stayed quiet, knowing exactly why.

Things came to a head when I found out what was really going on with Maine Maine and Sarah. So, I decided to take control. All the guys who had been hanging out across the hall, the ones who were always trying to talk to me, hit on me, or smoke, I invited them all over. I called about five guys, and we were all hanging out in the apartment, smoking, playing music, just chilling. Maine Maine walked in and immediately saw what was going down.

He was furious, yelling, "What the hell do you think you're

doing?"

I said, "The same thing you were doing when I was locked up—having a good time."

That's when he went off. He started cursing, telling me, "I think any of these guys are going to save you? Ain't nobody gonna save a hoe. I'll beat the shit out of you, and them, too. They ain't gonna do shit." At that point, one guy got up and ran, leaving four others behind. The other guys looked uncomfortable, and one by one, they all bailed. It was just me and him.

Maine Maine pushed one of the guys, and that guy got knocked out cold. He ran off. Then another guy slapped Maine Maine, and Maine Maine slapped him right back. That guy took off, too. Only one guy was left, and he just dipped out as well. So, now it was just me and Maine Maine in the apartment. The last guy to leave was me—sitting there, completely shocked. Out of five guys, not one of them could stand up to this messed-up coke head. It was crazy.

He lunged at me, and I tried to get out of the way, but it didn't work. He hit me hard, knocked me straight to the ground, and then started kicking me. He kicked me a few times and punched me, probably four or five times, before he stopped.

Then he said, "If I ever do this shit again, it's going to be worse."

At that moment, I knew I was really in a dangerous place. Things had gone too far. After that incident, the two girls who had moved out—the gay couple, Chelsea and her girlfriend— were still coming around sometimes. They'd show up at night, and all they'd do is get high, staying up until 3 or 4 in the morning with the music blasting and chaos going on. Maine Maine had left for a couple of days, but we all knew it was to cheat on me. He told me he was going to Oakshire, but I knew better.

Chelsea had stayed over at Felipe's apartment that night, her and her girlfriend. I knew things weren't good, but there was nothing I could do about it.

Chelsea had given this guy money for dope, and he took off with it. She was losing her mind, pacing around and cursing, not knowing what to do. Normally, I would've told her to take it as a loss and stop being an idiot. I don't hand over money to someone before I get the product. But instead, I said, "Give me the phone. Give me his number."

So I called the guy, pretending I needed to get served. When he showed up, I told Chelsea, "Come out now." As soon as he saw her, he knew what was up.

I walked up to him and said, "Give me her fucking money."

He looked confused and said, "You're her bitch?. You're not gay, are you?"

I looked him dead in the eyes and said, "No, that's my hope. Now give me my fucking money back."

He hesitated, then said, "Damn, I don't want no problems."

I told him, "You don't want any problems, I better get her money back."

He handed over $50, and I said, "That's all I want. Don't serve her again."

He agreed, saying, "I got you, I got you. I don't want no part of this."

I gave him a nod of appreciation, and he drove off. Chelsea came running down the stairs, thanking me like I was some kind of hero.

She was like, "I can't believe you stood up to him like that!" But in my head, I knew it wasn't about standing up to people.

It was about standing my ground. People will let you walk all over them if you let them. But I wasn't going to be that person.

After that, things kept spiraling, and Felipe was about to get kicked out. We had nowhere to go, so I applied for my own place at the same apartment complex. I got approved, but we both knew I didn't have the money to pay for it because I wasn't working. Maine Maine gave me the money, and I put it in my name.

I'll never forget that day. I was meeting Maine Maine to get the money order, and when he handed it to me, he spit in my face and called me a dirty bitch. He accused me of talking to Felipe and whatever else was going on in his head. The whole time, I just thought, how could you accuse me of talking to someone else when you've been out there cheating on me? He wouldn't even help make my bond, but when he was locked up, I still took care of him.

I realized something right then. If I could do all that for someone I loved, then any man could do it too. A real man, someone who wants you, is going to take care of you. They're going to put in the effort, make the time, and invest in the relationship. They're going to show you that they love you through their actions. But that wasn't happening with Maine Maine , and that was something Papa Lee taught me.

After I got the money order, I went over to get the stuff. At that point, I was just using him to get what I needed. When I moved into the apartment, I called him to come help. He showed up with a couple of guys, and that's when the situation really escalated.

So, Maine Maine had just left when Tim Tim showed up. Tim Tim and a few others were there—maybe three guys, I can't remember exactly who—but it was tense. Maine Maine showed up while they were still there, and they got into it. Words were exchanged, and Maine Maine went upstairs. That's when things started to go south.

Once he came up, everything blew up. We had a huge fight. The kind that gets out of control. I was just moving in, so I didn't have much, and it got physical. Furniture was knocked over, glass broke, and the situation only got worse. After that fight, things calmed down, and we went to bed. He went to work the next day, and I went to get Chase.

I was in contact with Alicia's family at the time—Mauricio, Benito, and the rest. They were workers and painters, and whenever I applied for a job, I'd get paycheck stubs made, using them or my sister for verification.

So the next day, I had Chase with me. We spent the day out, maybe at a pumpkin patch or something like that. Afterward, I dropped him back off and went back to the apartment, where Maine Maine was already waiting. He had started another argument, this time about the previous night. Then he beat me up again, locking me in the bathroom before setting the apartment on fire.

He thought I was dead. But somehow, I managed to break out of the bathroom, climb out of the second-story window, and jump down. I was bruised, and the smoke had already started to choke me. With no phone to call for help—because he'd taken it—I started walking from Spottswood to Olive Branch.

I walked the whole way. While I was walking, the fire department showed up to put out the fire, but they couldn't find me. They called my sister and she called my uncle Mauricio. They got in touch with the police, who said they had found a woman in the apartment and were trying to locate me, but they feared I was dead.

I didn't know what happened, but I do know this: by the time I walked through Goggy's door, she was shocked to see me. She had heard I was dead. She touched me to make sure I was real, asking me how I was alive. I told her how I jumped out of the window and walked all the way there. She rushed to get me a bath, called my sister, and told her I was alive. I'll never forget her reaction, how relieved she was, and how she took care of me when I needed it the most.

So, yeah, I guessed it. I had to move back in with Mama May, and Pops. They always made sure there was room for their kids, no matter how many there were. So, I moved back in with them. But even though I was back there, I was still working on getting my own place. I knew I didn't want to stay there for too long and be a burden. I was already the black sheep of the family, and the last thing I wanted was to be a burden on them, too.

12

Kingsgate

Fast forward to when I was at Lucy's house, and Maine Maine was still in Hillview. That's when Kingsgate came into the picture. KC was still around, doing her thing. I had worked at Olive Garden to get the pay stubs I needed for our plan, but things went sour with that job, so I had to scrap it. But Maine Maine knew the plan. He came to me one day and told me that he had secured the apartment we wanted. He'd done everything we'd talked about—he got the three-bedroom place, so KC could move in and even have her kids on the weekends. It was everything we needed. So that's how I ended up at Kingsgate.

When we moved into the apartment, things with him were still volatile, especially after everything with Cedric. He was beating me badly in Kingsgate, and I didn't tell Lucy because I didn't want her to think I was failing or prove her right, like, "I told YOU so." I just wanted to make it work. I wanted to have my own place, my own life, like my parents had—something I could call mine. I was trying so hard to make everything look okay, but deep down, I knew it wasn't.

Lucy could tell something was off. She noticed the locks on

the outside of the door that kept me trapped inside the room. I couldn't leave the room, much less the apartment. One time, he beat me so badly that I ended up in ICU for three days. I was there for a week in total. I was bruised up, battered—just completely destroyed. I remember calling Lucy, and she came, no questions asked. No matter what was going on between us, no matter how mad or upset we were with each other, she always showed up. That meant everything to me.

When I finally got out of the hospital, I told myself I was done. I packed up my things and told him I was leaving, just like before. This time, I went to Lucy's place, telling him I'd be back. He didn't believe me, though. He was convinced I was leaving for good.

I said, "How can I leave you when my stuff's still here?" But honestly, it didn't matter. My parents never gave me anything of real value, and the things I had didn't mean much to me. I could always replace things.

I went with Lucy, and it didn't take long before I came back. Things were still tense, but we were getting by. He tried to pull me back into his space, forcing me to watch movies with him, but I would just fall asleep on the couch. The cycle was the same. He'd go to work in the mornings and lock the door behind him, but one day, he didn't go to work. He told me he had business to take care of and was waiting on some people.

He had furnished the apartment from top to bottom—everything was set up: couches, lamps, I name it. We'd gone to furniture stores together, and I'd pick things out, but when I chose the expensive items, he would complain, asking why I wanted all the costly things. He was always beating my eyes out, and when I came home from the hospital, he begged me not to leave. He had paid the bills, bought all this furniture.

He said, "Please don't leave me. I'm doing everything for you."

But the reality was, I was still locked in that room. He thought the furniture would make things better, but I wasn't even able to enjoy it. I couldn't even go to the dentist. I was stuck in a situation I knew wasn't going to work, no matter how much I tried.

I didn't know it at the time, but KC and Maine Maine had something going on the whole fucking time while I was in rehab.

The second time I had went crazy and Maine Maine took me along with KC because they were trying to make me seem like I was crazy. I told them I wasn't going to Lakeside. I wasn't going here; I wasn't going there; the only place left that I said that I would go was La Paloma. I honestly needed time to think and I didn't know where else to go or what else to do. He was willing to pay for it so why not? When he dropped me off, at first I was thinking they're gonna kick me out in two or three days. There's no way he's gonna come up here with $1200, so they'll keep me so that he can get a break and that's exactly what he did.

When he did that, that's when I met Jay. Jay was an upper class black man his parents were pretty financially stable, but he just couldn't get his life together. To be honest, he never really was a druggie or into drugs. He was just confused running around with the wrong crowd that was trying to use him; nobody was ever genuine to him and nobody was ever real friend to him. I noticed that real quickly and that's when I chose to become a real friend to him and be kind. It ended up being a long time friendship that would last forever.

One time, I was still hanging out with Lucy and her nephew,

and things got bad again. He had locked me in the room, but I managed to sneak some of his stuff down from the second floor to the first, so Lucy's nephew could put it in his car. That way, I could get out for a little bit. When he came home and saw the door locked but me not in the room, he freaked out.

He was like, "How the hell did I get out? I locked you in so you couldn't leave."

I told him I just needed a little time away, but he wasn't having it. He wanted to know where his weed was.

I had taken it—smoked all of it. I gave half to my dad and half to Terry, and me, Lucy, and Terry smoked the rest. When I came back, he was furious.

He asked me, "Where's my weed?"

I said I didn't know, and that set him off. He immediately knew I was behind it, and that's when he slapped me.

He hit me so hard that my head hit the floor, and I couldn't even feel my face. It was like everything went numb, and all I could hear was a ringing in my ear. It was bad. He took my phone away, and I had to find a way to sneak and call Lucy.

When I finally reached her, she was upset. "Girl, You're crazy. I knew smoking all that weed would get you in trouble. I should have just left and come back. You don't need that weed to hang out with me."

I told her, "It's not that. He just pissed me off so bad, I had to do something to get back at him."

She was firm with me: "That ain't the way to handle it. I'm coming over tomorrow to check on you, but I don't want to see you like this.

" She told me to let the swelling go down, and I agreed.

Eventually, I moved back to Lucy's house. She was friends with a girl named Kariel, who had dated Terry in the past. That automatically made Kariel kind of off-limits, I guess, but I didn't have a problem with her, but she had a problem with me and I never understood why. It turned out it was just because I was the new one in the picture.

One time, me and Lucy were talking, and I said, "So what would happen if me and her got into it?"

Lucy just looked at me like I was crazy and said, "What makes you think you're my best friend?" That took me off guard. I had always thought we were best friends, but I didn't know if she felt the same way.

Then Lucy said, "Duh, why else would I be living with me? Of course, you're my best friend, girl. You're more like my sister."

That made me feel a lot better, but then I asked, "Well, what happens if she comes over to get her hair braided and we end up fighting? I know she doesn't like me."

Lucy didn't miss a beat and said, if we get into it, you just get into it. But if she starts winning, I'm jumping in too. Ain't nobody beating my friend."

From that point on, I knew where I stood with Lucy. We had each other's backs, no matter what. And I knew I'd always do the same for her.

13

Riverside

Running around Riverside was a mix of good days and bad days. Every day wasn't a win, and every encounter wasn't guaranteed money. Tricks could be as unreliable as anyone else, sometimes even worse. At least with some women, you 1 take their word, but a lot of the men out there were no better. They'd promise to "do right" or pay up, but after I held up my end, some didn't even want to pay. That's what brought out the uglier side of me. If you weren't going to give me what I came for after I did my part, then I'd take what was owed—whether it was weed, jewelry, or whatever else I could get my hands on to make it even.

During that time, I was bouncing back and forth between living with Tony and trying to keep it together while attending Christian Brothers University's nursing school at night. I remember walking everywhere—sometimes miles—just to keep things moving. By then, I had connections in the community, especially with the Iranians who owned several stores. I'd helped many of them pass their citizenship tests—store owners from Hillview, South Parkway, Poplar, and Cooper Young. They trusted me, and in return, they'd help me out when I needed something. If I needed a laptop for school, they'd say, "Help me pass the test, and I'll get it for you." It was all about exchange.

At Christian Brothers, I met this guy named Terrence. He always sat in the back and stayed to himself. He was pretty quiet, but he was like me I guess. We both get that from being antisocial, but that's also how we kind of bonded. He noticed that I needed a lot of help and he never minded helping me. When it came to things that I needed, just in life, he became a good friend and was somebody that I thank God that I met. He really became one of my good friends and I will never take our friendship for granted.

I'd tutor for hours, but I made sure I got what I needed. "I need $100 and some food from the store," I'd tell them. That's how I managed to eat, cover basic needs, and get gas. Whatever cash I had left would go toward cigarettes, weed, or even a hotel room. My go-to spot was the Regency Inn on Third Street. I rented rooms there so often that I formed a friendship with the staff. The manager, Melissa, knew me well. If I was short on cash, I'd explain, and she'd let me stay on credit, knowing I'd pay it back by cleaning rooms or picking up trash around the property.

Regency was my refuge, but I never brought men there. It was just a place to lay my head. Some days, I'd stay with Lucy, but I never overstayed my welcome. I'd spend a few nights there, then get a room for the rest of the week to give people space. I didn't want anyone to feel overwhelmed by me. Hell, my own family couldn't stand to be around me for more than thirty minutes—how could these strangers care enough to help me? That question haunted me, but I appreciated their kindness more than I could ever express.

I had also met Big Moe, the owner of three different phone stores—one in Bartlett, one in East Memphis, and another in Orange Mound. His uncles owned stores at both Wolfchase and Southland Mall. Big Moe knew the kind of stuff I was into because he was involved in similar things. He was two years younger than me but already had his life set up. His family used him to bring in money, so he had the resources to start whatever he wanted. The problem was, he could never stick to one thing for long. Every couple of years, he'd switch things up at his Orange Mound store.

One day, after I got a laptop, I needed to pay my phone bill but couldn't even get into the laptop. I told Big Moe about it, explaining that the laptop was supposed to be for school, but it was useless to me in its current state.

He said, "Bring it to me, Cry Baby. I'll reset it so you can use it for school."

I asked how much it would cost, and he said $60. I agreed because paying $60 for a $300 laptop I desperately needed was worth it. That interaction kicked off our friendship.

When I say "friendship," I mean we'd talk often but never hung out or did anything physical. Big Moe offered a couple of times, but I think he was more curious about how I'd respond. I never got the sense that he was truly interested; it was more like he wanted to know if he could have me if he tried.

There was a time when Tony cheated on me. I came home one day and found my dog outside. Furious and heartbroken, I tore up the apartment. Eventually, I moved back to Lucy's house, where I met Dre. He was cool—really cool. We connected on a simple "Can I get your number? I like the way you look" vibe. He liked me for real and wanted a relationship, but deep down, I knew I couldn't give him that. I wasn't ready. I was still trying to find my way and get out of the mess I was in.

Dre and I clicked. He'd pick me up, drop me off, and we just vibed. One night, I didn't have anywhere to stay, so he took me to his dad's house where he was living. Dre had just gotten out of jail three months earlier, saved up, and bought himself a Lexus. We went to his room, got into bed, and... nothing happened. The connection felt so off, but we didn't even need to talk about it. We both agreed silently: if we crossed that line, we'd ruin what we had.

What we had was solid. It wasn't a romantic relationship; it was more like a brother-sister bond. We looked out for each other. He'd come over to my mom and dad's house to smoke or hang out, and we just kept things cool. Over time, I started opening up to him more.

One day, I told Dre I needed money, but I couldn't go to a bank because I didn't have any legal income.

He told me, "Man, let me introduce you to my dad. He'll take care of you."

At first, I didn't know what he meant. Then I met his dad, who everyone called Pops.

Pops wasn't just anybody. He was well-known and respected—a shot-caller. He didn't do the work himself; he had people to handle things for him. But he was no joke. The deal was simple: for every $50 you borrowed, you paid back $75 in a week. If it took two weeks, you owed $100. It was steep, but at the time, I needed it. I had to get by—shampoo, tampons, pads, clothes, and just the basics to survive.

I didn't always know where I'd be sleeping that night, maybe a hotel if I could swing it, or back at Papa Lee's house if I had nowhere else. No matter what, I knew I could always go there. It was safe, and that was all I needed at the time.

Before Tony cheated on me, back when I was walking to school every day. he made sure I always had someone with me when he wasn't around, almost like a security detail, though I didn't realize it at the time.

I began transitioning from Tony's house back to Papa Lee's, it felt like a cycle I couldn't escape. Returning home was a painful reminder that I hadn't succeeded, that I was stuck right back where I started. By then, I had lost my car—a consequence of karma, I suppose, for the things I did just to survive. Some days, I'd set up dates with strangers just to have a meal. I'd sit quietly, eat like a lady, and leave. No one ever knew what I was going through because I never told anyone.

Things were so bad I'd even learned how to steal and reinstall electric meters. One time, I grabbed a meter off a gas station on Highland, near the railroad tracks. Behind it were three apartment complexes, and I picked three meters—just in case one failed, I'd have backups. That was how I survived.

Hank and I had been through so much together that it created a bond between us. We didn't need to explain things; we just understood. If I needed something, he'd get it, and if he needed help, I'd do what I could. It wasn't a romantic relationship—it was a trauma bond.

One night, we were driving around with three meters in the trunk. I told Hank I didn't want to stay in the hood—I wanted to stay somewhere nice for once.

He laughed and said, "How are we going to do that without the neighbors calling the cops on us?" He was right; it would've been obvious we didn't belong.

Instead, we got realistic. We drove to Castalia, broke into a house, and installed a meter. I took a shower and lay down while Hank stayed up all night, hustling on the phone: getting guns dropped off, setting up deals, and finding ways to get cash. Whatever money he made, he gave me so I could eat.

We were both doing whatever we could to make it another day. I wasn't any better than him; I was just as broken. The only people who cared were Lucy and her parents, but relying on them made me feel like being a burden. My own family didn't care, at least it felt that way. They never called to check if I was okay or even asked if I'd eaten. If they'd ever reached out and told me to come home, to start over, I would've run back in a heartbeat, but they didn't, so I kept going.

Being homeless felt like being invisible. Sure, Lucy's parents helped when they could, but it wasn't the same as having a real home. I stopped caring about the risks I took because, honestly, I wasn't scared of dying. I was scared of living. Dying would've been easier, cheaper. But every day, I fought to stay alive, even when it felt like the world didn't care. Living is the hardest thing I've ever done.

There was this time we were living at Lucy's house, and in the neighborhood, there was this guy named Luke who had everything: the drugs, the money, the cars, the guns, the whole package. He was known around the area. I wouldn't say he was all that, but to me, he was something else. Everything about him was different, in a way that felt so out of reach. But when it came to Terry, it was a whole different story. Terry wasn't about the money or the drugs; he had something real. It wasn't about the stuff—he connected with me on a soul level. It was love, true love, and I didn't need anything else. Even now, though Terry isn't with me, what we had will never be the same again.

14

Kirby Parkway

During Cedric's incarceration I extended an olive branch by trying to help Cedric's two cousins. Their mom had kicked them out because they weren't interested in getting jobs, and I could relate to being in that situation. I knew what it felt like to have nowhere to go, so I offered to let them stay with me on the condition that they get jobs. By then, Chicago had switched from dealing heroin to weed, so I was getting weed from him to sell. I figured I could put weed in their pockets to help them make money. They could sell it, keep some for themselves, and put money aside to eventually get their own place.

After I moved into the apartment off of Kirby, I made it my own. I had Cedric's cousin, Josh, paint the walls. He's an amazing artist and a tattoo artist, so I knew he'd do a great job. He drew the Ninja Turtles on the wall, and I decked the place out with all things Ninja Turtle—curtains, lights, sheets, I name it. The bathroom was all Batman-themed. My bedroom was midnight blue with black and white decor, and the den was all red with white furniture. That was the first apartment Josh and I got together. I put it in my name, but Josh covered the bills.

The other cousin ended up moving in with his white girl-friend. Before they moved out, she had an issue with me. At the time, I had broken my foot, but they were moving into their new apartment, which was just a street over. I was getting rid of some old furniture because Josh had bought me new stuff, and I offered to give them what I didn't need to help them furnish their new place. I had never had anything new before, everything I owned was used. His girlfriend had an issue, and I think she thought I was trying to get with her boyfriend, which wasn't true. I had no interest in him, he was just helping me out. She confronted me about it, and things escalated.

She insisted we fight, but I was like, "I have a broken foot, I'm not fighting you." Lucy, who was with me, suggested we go outside to handle it, thinking she could jump in if needed.

We fought, and I was winning, but when I was getting up, she pulled a knife and cut me. Lucy tried to intervene, but the guys held her back, letting the girl continue to attack me. I managed to kick her off, but in retaliation, she stabbed my two back tires, flattening them. Afterward, her cousins came by to check on me. They acted like they were on my side, but I knew they had just let it all happen. Big Mike, one of the cousins still staying with me, was also acting like he didn't mess with them, but deep down, I knew something wasn't right.

At this point, Cedric's cousins had their own place, and I had mine. My cousin, Rosalee, was still living with me at the time, along with her dog. That night, she and her dog went to my grandmother's house, and I stayed home with Chase. One of the cousins pretended he was going to work, even though he was really just sleeping on the couch. He locked the door and left, but he tipped off the others, telling them that I was alone with my son and that they should go ahead and rob us. I had a broken foot and was still recovering from the fight I'd had a few days earlier. When they came in, two of them had their faces covered, but one didn't. I was shocked. I couldn't believe they were robbing me, especially when I was hurt and with my son in the room. I tried to stand my ground, but they didn't care. They told me to get under the bed, but I couldn't fit with my foot the way it was, and I wasn't about to crawl under there in front of my son. They didn't care. They told me to wake Chase up and put both of us in the closet while they took everything.

They took my gun, my jewelry, my credit cards, and even the cable boxes and remote controls. The whole place was cleared out, but they didn't tie me up properly and I managed to get Chase out. I told him to go to the neighbors for help. He was scared, but I told him to be brave. He banged on the door until Tracy, the neighbor, finally let him in and called 911. While the police were on their way, I stayed in the closet, devastated by what had happened.

When the police arrived, I told them exactly who had done it and where they lived. They took me and Chase in the back of the squad car and went straight to their house. The police officers pretended to be doing a wellness check, but they used the opportunity to walk right in when they saw the door was cracked open. Inside, they found all the stolen items. The guys tried to play it cool, but they slipped up. One of the officers pointed out that their story didn't make sense, and they got caught in their lies.

I had receipts for all of my stuff and ended up getting back what they could return—most of it, anyway. The gun was never recovered. The thieves went to jail, and I made sure they stayed there for as long as possible, attending every court date and pushing for them to serve their full sentence. After a few days, my ex reached out, asking me to come over. I found out he was at their place, and it's clear they might be trying to set me up again. But I'm done with them. I'm not letting them get to me.

I didn't stay in that apartment long, maybe about a year. Family started coming around more often, and by then, I was still on and off with Bobby. Terry and I were supposed to be seeing each other exclusively. That was the same year Terry passed away—on his birthday, actually.

A lot of things happened in that apartment. Josh got caught stealing from the casino, which is how he'd been paying for everything—furniture, jewelry, everything I wanted. I had no idea. He was caught stealing $75,000, and that's when I found out how he'd been supporting our lifestyle. Lucy's niece was the one who tipped her off, and Lucy told me. When Josh came home and told me, I was completely shocked.

He explained that his job involved clearing out machines that collected tickets, and he had been taking the ones with the most money on them. He was cashing them out, finding people to exchange them for him, and then keeping most of the money for himself. He'd been sharing some of the money with another woman, who got caught and ratted him out. That's how everything came to light.

To make matters worse, he had been giving me stolen tickets as well, telling me he won them at work during his lunch break. He never told me they were stolen, so I ended up cashing in faulty tickets without knowing they were illegal. I thought he was just letting me keep the cash or use the tickets as I wanted. I was completely blindsided by the whole thing.

15

Smokey City

Sharyn was always around when I had heroin. She would want to test it to make sure it was good, since she knew I needed to verify it before selling it to anyone else. She got free heroin from me, which kept her close. Eventually, Sharyn started dating a guy named Mang, thinking he was the one providing the heroin. However, Mang didn't even know I had the heroin until Sharyn told him. When he found out, he went through all my things and took everything. At this point, I was left with nothing—no heroin and no way to make money—but Sharyn was still there, high as could be, and everything had been taken from me.

Sharyn was also involved with another drug dealer named Sugar Bear, who knew a guy named Bobby. I needed to get more heroin, so I asked Sharyn to help me get it. I drove her to Smokey City in my car, which I'd gotten from someone named Jimmy. We met Sugar Bear there, and I took the chance to talk to him. I needed to get my car back, which had been taken by my boyfriend, and Sugar Bear gave me Bobby's number. I explained the situation to Bobby over the phone and told him

I wasn't playing around—I needed to get things straightened out. I made it clear I didn't want to meet at any trap houses; I wanted him to meet me at my apartment to show him I was serious.

Bobby came over to my place. When he arrived, we had a tense conversation. I needed to let him know I wasn't messing around. We both had guns, but I told him I just wanted to talk. As we sat down, I asked him how he knew Sugar Bear. He explained that Sugar Bear had sent him to do some work for me. I told him I wasn't looking for a job done—I needed to get my heroin back. Bobby asked who I was after, and I told him there were three guys in a house who had my stuff. These guys were part of the group that Luke, a guy I knew from Riverside, hung out with. Luke was one of the people who had taken my heroin, and now I needed to get it back.

Jimbo and Sugar Bear used to run around together and one day, I was hanging with them. I had a lot of Xanax that I needed to get off because Bobby was getting them in by the boatloads. We were both doing our own thin trying to sell it. I pulled up to Lee St. but Sugar Bear wasn't there this time.

He was like "Just go up there. They're gonna buy em. They're gonna buy em"

So I go up there and I was intimidated as fuck, but I just held my head high. As I got to the door, there were four or five guys just jumping at the opportunity to talk to me. They asked what did I want, what was I there for, please tell them that I would never leave, just all of the things. This guy named Jimbo came to the front.

I called Sugar Bear back and was like, "Who am I looking for ? Who do I need to talk to?"

He said, 'Just tell them you're looking for Jimbo," so I told him that.

Jimbo brought me in the back and we discussed business. We took care of the pills, but we also made sure that we were straight. I was never gonna change prices on him or switch up. We were locked in and he had my back. Anything I needed or wanted, I was straight; he was just a phone call away and that was for anything. Come to find out, what a small world because that was the friend my sister would have drinks with at the bar after work.

During the time I was staying at Sharyn's house, occasionally spending nights at Bobby's, and still in on-and-off contact with Maine Maine, life was chaotic. Maine Maine had his suspicions about me being involved with his dad, but I never confirmed or denied it. Meanwhile, Josh was around frequently, and we were always busy with one thing or another.

Amidst all this, I met a girl named Tiffany. We crossed paths when I was at the store looking for hair products that weren't available. Later, I went to Supercuts on Winchester to get Chase's haircut, and there she was, working there. We struck up a conversation, and I asked for her number, mentioning that I preferred getting my hair done privately rather than at the shop. Tiffany was friendly and gave me her number, telling me she did both men's and women's hair at her house.

Tiffany was a whirlwind of energy—completely unique. From the start, she was honest about her lifestyle.

She said, "I do dope. I mean, I shoot up."

I appreciated her honesty and said, "That's fine, as long as you don't pressure me. I just smoke weed." She was cool with that, and we began hanging out often. Sometimes, I'd even stay the night at her place before heading back to Sharyn's.

At this point, Tiffany's kids were living with her ex-husband, so it was just her in her home on South Cox. She had a room with its own entrance, which made coming and going easy. Eventually, she agreed to rent the room to me, and I stayed there for about three months. Things changed when she reconciled with her partner and needed the space for her boys, so I moved out.

Instead of going back to Mama May and Papa Lee's place, Josh helped me secure an apartment off Kirby. That's where things took a darker turn when Cedric's people robbed Chase and me.

Despite everything, Tiffany was always good to join in on a couple of sessions. The most I had to do was let him rub my feet, even between my toes. He paid $400, so I figured, why not? Strangely, I discovered I liked it. I hate feet usually, but there was something about it that turned me on. It felt weird, but it was a weird discovery about myself.

When I had to move out of Tiffany's house, Josh helped us get an apartment off Kirby. Tiffany once told me about how a doctor who wasn't even certified did her breast surgery, and it didn't go well. She warned me that if I ever got surgery, I should make sure the doctor was certified. I didn't really think much about it at the time, but it's something I remember now.

Tiffany's husband moved in time. We'd go out in Midtown, starting with buying our first drink, and soon enough, we'd have men offering to buy the rest. Sometimes, we'd invite them back to her place on South Cox, where we'd continue the party. Sometimes it was just drinks and conversation; other times, it was more.

I remember one time a chef came over; he was a professional chef, and the next morning, he left after everyone had fallen asleep. It was one of those moments that seemed too crazy to be real, but it actually happened. I know, the kind of thing I see in movies and think would never happen in real life—but it does. Some people just want to have a good time, and if they have the means to make that happen, they do. Money can relieve stress and let people have fun without worrying about anything else.

I had some crazy experiences with this girl I was close to. She had this guy from Denver who was paying her for services, but she invited me back in, and I ended up moving back into my apartment off Kirby. About six months later, I visited Tiffany and her boys for dinner, and we watched a movie together. It was one of those little moments I still cherish. Then one day, I texted her husband to check in, and he told me some devastating news. Tiffany had gone to meet some people for drugs, and they found her body on Allen Rd in North Memphis. She was unrecognizable, but they said she fought back—there were signs of it, like skin under her nails. She had been robbed, dragged in, assaulted, and ultimately left to die. I was in shock. I couldn't believe it.

It really messed me up for a while. I saw her husband, Danny, and he gave me a few of Tiffany's belongings. I still have them today, along with a few things from other people, like Sharyn. Those few things are what make up my personal collection now. But Tiffany's death hit me hard. It was a harsh reality I'll never forget.

Sharyn lost everything to drugs. She was around me for a while, still hanging on to a bit of money, but this is when I completely stopped dealing with her. I had to undergo a surgery to remove cysts from my uterus, and she was the only one there for me at the time. She drove me to the hospital in my car and picked me up after the surgery.

Before the surgery, they make me take off all my jewelry. I

had one necklace with three charms and another with a cross on it, both gifts from my First Communion. They were the few things I had that meant a lot to me, given to me by Granny Edra and Goggy. When I woke up from the surgery, my jewelry was gone. Sharyn had stolen it. I knew it was gone because she had a habit of pawning things for drugs. I never saw those pieces again.

Now, fast forward to me living in an apartment off Kirby. Sharyn was at her lowest point. She didn't have a car, just some clothes and her purse with drugs in it. She had about $20,000 left in the bank, and she asked me to help her get $7,000 worth of dope. She offered me $20 to go do it, but by then, I was done with her. She had taken from me one too many times. She had stolen my jewelry, used me, and I couldn't take it anymore.

At the time, I didn't have a car, but my sister had just gotten a white Jeep Cherokee. She let me borrow it while she was at work. I told Lucy that I wasn't going to help her anymore, and when she insisted, I told her I was going to rob her. She asked me what the plan was, and I didn't have one.

I said, "I need to figure it out," and I told her I'd text her once I got there.

We drove to a store in Riverside, and Lucy said her friend Michy would act like he had the dope. He'd pull a gun on us and rob us. It seemed like a set-up, but at that point, I didn't care. I just wanted to be done with her.

When we pulled up, Michy came to the window and said, "Give me the purse, give me the money." Sharyn hesitated, but I told her to hand it over, that I didn't want anyone to die over this. She handed him the purse, and we sped off.

Back at her house, we met up with her brother, and they went to get the money. Afterward, they came back, and we all checked the purse. It had dope, money, and other stuff in it. Lucy and her brother decided to split the money three ways. We took $3,000 each, and we gave $1,000 to Papa Lee, since everything had gone down at his house. We all walked away with a little something to get back on our feet.

Afterward, I had to pick up my sister in her car. I told her what happened, that I had robbed someone using her car. She couldn't believe it at first, but I wanted her to hear it from me, not someone else. She dropped me back off at Sharyn's place, and then I left. I also gave her some money before I left, even though things had gone south with Sharyn.

At one point, I met Tony, another chef, and he introduced me to the owner of Babalu. So, I started going to Midtown for drinks and things like that while Bobby was at work. But things weren't all smooth. I eventually caught Bobby talking to other girls, and when I confronted him, he'd stop for a bit but always went back to the same behavior. We were together for about six months, and during that time, I was still trying to figure out if I should stay or leave.

Tony always hung out with a group of three guys: Hank, Claude, and Big D. Big D had a nephew, whom we called the "baby" because he was the youngest of the group. They were always around, even if Bobby wasn't, and they'd be there as a kind of backup for each other. But because I was around, they looked out for me, too. Hank was always there, especially when Tony wasn't. I'd find myself spending a lot of time at the house with Hank, and we'd talk. He'd talk about his women, and I'd talk about Tony.

One day, Hank told me, "I don't know why you let him treat you like this. I know he cheats on you, right?"

He also mentioned how I was often the one helping Tony with

his drug problems.

"You're the one with the connection," he said. "Why don't you just do your own thing?"

I explained that I couldn't, because as a woman in that world, all I'd ever be was a "little white girl" to people, and I wasn't going to negotiate my prices. I told him, "When I deal with Black people, they don't respect your prices. They want to haggle or make deals, and I don't do that. I know what I want, and they know what they want. Either they're willing to pay, or they're not. I'm not here to negotiate. If they want to deal, great. If not, they can walk away."

Hank seemed surprised by my perspective and said, "Damn, I never thought of it like that."

Hank looked at me and said, "You know Tony's still cheating on you, right?"

I nodded. "I know, but he says he's stopped, so who knows?" I replied.

"Man, he hasn't stopped," Hank said, shaking his head.

I sighed and said, "Yeah, but until I catch him again, there's not much I can do about it. I have to trust him for now, or it's all just a waste." Hank seemed to get it. "Yeah, I feel that," he said.

One night, Tony was working, and things were so bad. We were completely broke—no cigarettes, no food, nothing. We were waiting for him to get home because, being a chef, he could bring some food back with him. But I was fed up. I grabbed my laptop, which was practically a piece of junk, and I decided I had to sell it. We needed the money. So Hank and I walked to two gas stations on Lamar Rd, trying to get rid of this laptop. We probably looked like a mismatched pair—me and Hank walking down the street, me trying to get rid of this laptop, and Hank just looking tough.

The thing with Hank was, he had this intimidating look. He wasn't shy about showing he could be mean, and people could tell. So when we'd approach someone, they'd get scared, lock their doors, roll up the windows, and ignore us.

I told Hank, "Stop scaring people off. Let me do it. I need you to be my security, that's it." He agreed, though he was a little skeptical.

I walked up to the first person, and after a short conversation, I sold the laptop for $300. Hank and I walked back to the apartment laughing the whole way, amazed that it actually worked. We were feeling pretty good about it, considering the situation.

At this point, I wasn't really talking to anyone in my family, but Rosalee and I were still in touch. She'd been living in Texas, but we kept up our friendship through calls and messages. As for Hank, we had gotten closer. We'd formed a strange bond, mostly due to all the times we were dealing with Tony's lies and me catching him in the act. Hank had even driven me to places where I caught Tony cheating on me. We kind of became friends, but I think deep down, we both knew there was something more between us.

By this point, things were getting even more intense. One morning, Hank was walking me to school. I had a .380 in my bag, and Hank was probably carrying a Glock or something similar. As we walked, I noticed Sharyn, someone I had robbed two years earlier, driving by.

She slowed down when she saw me and yelled, "I'm going to get you, bitch!"

I didn't think much of it at first, but then she made a U-turn. I turned to Hank and said, "She's coming back around for me. If they start shooting, stop and go the opposite direction. They'll be aiming where they think we're heading, but if we move the other way, they'll miss."

Sure enough, when she came back around, she let off three rounds—*pop pop pop.* I hit the pavement hard to avoid getting shot, scraping up my face in the process. Hank, though, didn't flinch. He stood his ground, ten toes down, and didn't move. That's when the real action started. Sharyn was "cloud shooting"—firing wildly without aim—but she didn't hit me. Hank, on the other hand, wasn't playing around. He fired four shots, and every single one hit her car. They took off so fast they didn't even think twice about messing with me again.

By the time I even thought about opening my bag to grab my gun, it was already over. Hank had handled everything. We decided not to risk staying on the same route in case they circled back, so we switched it up and ditched school for the day. Instead, we went back to the house, lit up, and tried to process everything. That morning was a close call, but after that, I knew Sharyn wasn't going to mess with me again.

After that, I never saw Sharyn again until about two years ago. I saw her on Park Ave, standing there, homeless and asking for change. It was strange to see how things had turned out for her.

16

Macon Road

At this point, my sister and I had never really lived together outside of our parents' house. I could sense that she never really wanted me there, but she understood I needed a place to stay, so she let me move in. By then, she had already moved to Atoka, and Marissa had left for Italy, so I was left alone in the house for the last month before I had to move out.

I had been in the process of looking for a new place to live. I had been trying to find something with Josh, applying to apartments and figuring out where we could go. I had already ruined my credit with a few previous apartments, including one at Kingsgate and another on Spottswood, both of which were either under other people's names or messed up due to situations beyond my control. I couldn't get anything under my own name anymore. Josh had a place on Kirby, and we'd left that apartment on good terms, so his credit wasn't impacted, but I wasn't going to get anywhere with my own applications. Eventually, we found a new place off Macon and Graham, across from the Stephenson's grocery store. That's when things started shifting.

My sisters were in Atoka, Tony and I weren't speaking, Bobby was in jail, and Cedric was off in Ohio with another woman, trying to build a new life. At this point, it was just me and Hank. Hank had a crew of three guys that were close-knit, and we'd become more like family than anything else. We spent a lot of time together, even though we didn't get close in a romantic or physical way. We had a routine, and everything felt comfortable.

As I moved into the new place, I told myself I was going to make this work. I set up a room for my son and planned to get him once a month, even though I knew that might not happen. I wasn't going to get caught up in old habits. I was determined to focus on a fresh start, even though I didn't know how things would unfold. This time, I wasn't going to let any men come over, and if they wanted to see me, we'd meet elsewhere. If we went to a hotel, it was strictly for business — drugs, no other distractions. No more tricks, only deals with sugar daddies, or so I told myself.

I focused on running things my way. Drugs became my primary focus. I wasn't using anymore, but I knew how to sell and that became my sole business. Hank and his crew helped with the logistics. We'd set up deals through Hank, who would keep me at a distance from the customers, passing information but never letting them get too close to me. I became known in the city for having the best product, the best prices, and the most efficient operation. I worked hard to keep everything smooth and anonymous, only interacting with those I trusted.

On top of the drug trade, I set up dates with men. My rules were strict: they would pay for everything, from babysitters to food, and I would make sure that the minimum for a date was $300. Some nights, I'd run five dates, making a good chunk of money in a short period of time. That was the goal — to make money without letting anything slip.

Despite the money, I wanted to keep my son out of this world. I didn't want him caught up in it, so I tried to keep the business separate, but life didn't always go as planned. I did what I had to do to survive, but at least this time, I was in control.

I appreciated that Hank was always on time. There's nothing worse than when someone pulls a stunt and leaves you waiting, especially when everything needs to be perfectly timed. If things weren't done right, it could all fall apart. For example, if the timing wasn't right with Thomas or my Uber, it could set everything off course.

The next thing I'd hear from the guy was, "I could give you a ride," and I knew exactly what that would lead to: "Do you want to go to my place or yours? Should we get a hotel?"

I wasn't interested in going down that route, so having him be punctual was crucial. I remember one specific time when things got really messed up. It was a mess, and I couldn't afford to let things slide like that again.

17

Cartel

After Macon I had moved to living on Verne St. The last month that I was there by myself; that's when I was getting in touch with my cousin Rosalee and she was living in Texas. She was living in Texas, and I was living in Memphis. She said that she would be coming down here on certain days and that she would want to see me then. We were always really close. Rosalee and I were close, and Karen and Marissa were close. I don't really know, but. It was like KiKi was close with everybody and then me and Veronica were close, too. But just me and Rosalee were always very close, probably because we are the babies, but also outcasts of their family.

Rosalee had came to my house and I said, "What are you doing down in Memphis? You've came down here two or three times at this point."

She had sent me money helping me out here and there with the light bill at KiKi's house, but in the end, I ended up leaving KiKi with the light bill that I didn't pay, though I did go back and pay her later.

I asked her, "How are you coming down to Memphis and

sending me money? Like, how are you doing on this?"

She said, "Well, I just want to help and I'm able to help others."

"Well, you're not making this much money at Denny's. What are you really doing?" I asked.

"I'm scared to tell you because I don't want to get you involved. And then. Things go left and I just don't know what to do. I just. I'm already in deep and I just don't want to get you in any deeper than I am," she replied.

I kept prodding her, "Well, what are you doing because I need to make money too? Whatever you're doing to make money, I need to do the same shit. So you know, I was selling heroin for money, but I haven't touched that shit in a while. And I want to do anything but pick that shit back up."

,"Well, shit, you know my dad, he he works with the cartel, so I'm working with the cartel!" she exclaimed.

"Well, fuck. What do you mean?" I asked.

"I mean, like I'm trafficking dope."

"Oh, my God, Rosalee, how long have you been doing this?"

"Well, I've only been doing it for maybe like six months now."

"How much have you made and went over the numbers and this and that? So what do you have to do?" I inquired.

She explained, "I don't know, sometimes I have to go to Louisiana. Sometimes I have to go to Texas, and I always have to go to Texas to get it. But then I have to drop it off in Atlanta. But sometimes I go through, you know, Memphis or Louisiana, this and that."

"You didn't pay to travel, you drop some shit off, and go back home and pay your bill be straight, so sounding good to me." I was gung ho.

She didn't want to do it alone anymore. She was needing help because when she was driving, her ankles were swelling up so bad that she was having to take an extra day or two at the hotel to relax and just prop her feet. But because of the drive in so she was kind of being late and on the trip she was being late on the trip. Well, with me and her driving together, she could drive halfway. I'd drive halfway and, BAM, we were knocking trips out. We were knocking trips out faster than she was alone. Then they were doubling up this shit on us; they were doubling up orders and it would just be more and more.

I would ask Rosalee, "How are you dealing with your mom?" because, as I have said, her mom was a crack head and she was in a prostitute. Melissa and Karen always hated me, and Melissa had a thing where she was racist and she didn't like the fact that I fucked black guys and she always called me a "nigga lover" and this and that. It was always something with me and a black guy, and she she hated me for that. Karen hated me for her son. Chris didn't like me because he touched me when I was younger and I told on him. I was the black sheep of the family and Marissa and I didn't really talk. She always did her own thing, separate from the family. So it was me and Rosalee. We have a super strong bond. I also had my sister, KiKi. I had Lucy and NeNe was there, but not really like that. She would be there here and there, just strictly for my kid.

At first Rosalee and I weren't making much. It would just be the numbers would just change. I can't even remember the numbers, but the numbers would just change. At first it would start off $5000 a piece, or the second time it would be $8000 a piece. It would just depend on what we were doing, how much we were doing, and where we were going; all of that factored in gas, hotels, all of that stuff.

At this point, Rosalee and I had made some trips. When we came back home, she wouldn't always stay at the house on Verne. Sometimes she would go to Goggy's house. At this time, I had this dog named Zoe. It was a poodle mixed with Yorkie. It was a "porky." I think they called it her Yorkiepoo or something like that. It looked like a Yorkie with all the colors, but with the crazy hair of a poodle. It was very obnoxious and just bounced around all the time. On one trip, Rosalee and I went on, we came back and something just felt eerie, like when we pulled up in the driveway. I don't know how to explain it, but something just felt wrong.

When we pulled up, I said, "Go in the house,"

She said, "Well, I'm not going in. First you go in. Why would I go in first?"

I said, "Because you're bigger, Rosalee. If you go in first and they kill you, that'll give me enough time to run away or call the police."

We both started laughing because I would always make jokes in serious situations or always make fun of, you know, whatever. I would always make jokes. I was always the funny one. She was like, "Oh my God, I'm gonna pee."

While we were still laughing, we went up to the doorstep together, and then I go back to the car and sit down and she goes in. It was kind of like I made her think we were going to go in together and I ran back to the car.

She explained, "So nothing's wrong, nothing's missing, but there's something really fucking weird and it's fucking off."

I asked, " What? What happened? Is Zoe in there?"

She said, "Zoe's dead, but the way that she died is kind of fucked up."

I said, "What?"

She said, "You know, that shirt, the memorial shirt you had made for Terry."

I said, "Yeah."

She said, "That shirt. Remember when we left, we hung it up because you have to hang it up to dry."

Again, I said, "Yeah."

She said, "You remember you hung it up on the bed and we left,"

I said, "Yeah, we locked up the house. We left. We went to Texas."

She said, "Right. I remember the same thing you remember. So we're on the same page."

And I said, "Yeah," and started laughing.

She said, "The dog is dead under the bed, like the bed collapsed, maybe, but the shirt is over the body but under the bed, so it's like the bed, the shirt, and then the dog, and then the floor. How the hell did this shirt get over the dog? And how the hell did the bed just collapse? A bed doesn't just collapse if you don't...You know what I mean? If you don't, if you don't have weight on it or nobody's like laid on it like you know, like it is just fucking weird."

We never knew why, but I ended up burying Zoe in the backyard and I planted a flower. There is a little grave off of Verne.

By that time I had told Goggy and she was like, "Oh, baby, don't you worry about it. You'll get another dog, but you have to wait. You know, you need time to get over that dog. 1st and plus, you don't really need a dog right now going back and forth."

I said, "Yeah. I know you're right. I probably don't need a dog right now anyway."

Rosalee and I did a couple more trips and there was nothing really fascinating about it. It wasn't the fast life, the drug life, but we did get pulled over one or two times. I remember one time we got pulled over and they looked in the back of our trunk and we had all the fucking dope in the back of the trunk. When they look in the back, they didn't see anything but candy.

They asked, "Why do y'all have so much candy?" The dope was in the candy; what they were doing was melting the candy down, putting the dope in and then re- hardening the candy and repackaging it back up. That's how we were traveling this shit. That's how everything was moving.

We didn't know it at the time because her dad told us that we had stopped doing dope and we were selling candy for pinatas, for parties and shit. But it was Mexican candy that they couldn't get over here, so we'd have to pick it up in Texas. We really thought we were having candy, though, come to find out that was what was really going on. So when we got pulled over, they looked at the candy. We told them that we had just picked it up from Texas so we could take it for pinatas to a party down in Atlanta for our aunt. They let us go and we kept going.

Another time we got pulled over, Rosalee and I, we had around $50,000 on us in cash and we had to open the car and they said the limit that we could have was $10,000. They took our fucking money and gave us $10,000 and let us go. They said, "Go on now. Pull off" and we just pulled the fuck off. Never spoke about it. Like what the fuck! They had just taken our money, so we had to explain that shit to the cartel. The cartel didn't want to hear that shit. Something got back to her dad, and I never really knew what happened to him, but I knew that they got him. They said that they pulled him out of his house and beat the shit out of him, but I don't really know because unless I see it for myself, I can't speak on it.

18

Castalia & Willett Street We Will Let Your Ass Have It

Now, it was just me, Hank, Big D, and the baby. Hank had a girlfriend, Debo, someone he was exclusive with. She was the first one he was really serious about, but he always ran back to her. No matter what, he would mess around with other women, but he'd always go back to Debo. The problem was, after he put his hands on her, she wasn't playing anymore. She always played mind games, doing things that would get him all riled up. In the end, it would piss everyone off, and he should've just left her alone, but he couldn't stop. We all have our weakness, and she was his.

At this point, Hank was out of town with Pooh Shiesty and Big 30. He was finally rubbing elbows with the right people—rappers, influencers, everyone he needed to know to get out of the life he was living. I was so proud of him for taking those steps for himself. With Hank gone, Big D, the baby, and I stepped up to fill his role, helping with security, watching the place, getting the money, and pulling up on people to drop things off. We took over the responsibilities Hank usually handled when he was out making moves.

One time, I had to head to Atoka because my sister was giving me some cash. By then, I had a van—my uncle Javier had a work van that he didn't need anymore after he got a new truck, so he sold it to me. It was a blue minivan, not exactly glamorous, but it worked. So, Big D and I were in the van, with the baby in the back seat. We all had cash on us, so money wasn't an issue.

But, of course, the police pulled up behind us. The tags were out of date because I had just bought the van and hadn't gotten new ones yet.

They pulled us over, and Big D immediately said, "Damn, I got the Draco on me."

I was like, "What?!?"

He repeated, "I got the Draco on me."

I couldn't believe it. "Fucking, Big D!" I said.

He wasn't joking. "Yeah, we finna go to jail," he added.

But I wasn't about to let that happen. The whole time the police were behind us, Big D and I were swapping seats. Now I was in the driver's seat, and he was in the passenger seat.

"I need to get out when they pull us out, and I need to do all the talking,"

Big D said. "I'm gonna get rid of the gun." I agreed, knowing that if things went sideways, I'd have to rely on him to get me out of this mess.

The police pulled us out of the car, and the officer started questioning me. I just kept talking, talking non-stop. The more I talked, the more the officer focused on me. When you're talking to someone, you're looking at them, and they can't see anything else. Meanwhile, Big D slid out of the passenger seat, casually walked to the back of the car, and threw the gun. He tossed it like it was nothing, walked to the back of the van, and acted like it never happened.

The officer saw him and immediately called out, "Hey, sir, come back here!"

But Big D kept walking, saying, "I'm getting out of the car." He played it cool, like nothing was out of the ordinary.

The officer took me to jail for driving with a suspended license. I left my purse and my keys with Big D, and told him to follow me to the jail. There is cash in my purse, pay the bond with that. They pulled with the van, got me out, and we went right back to where we had been pulled over, retrieved the gun (an AK47), and went on about our mission.

In December, Tina, my cousin Marissa's mom died. Tina was living at Goggy in Olive branch and she called me the night before Marissa took her to the hospital.

She wanted me to give her a ride that night and I said, "Tina I'm not doing it. I just got me a room and I need to settle in. I've got to relax. I've had a really funked up day I just came up with money just to get a room."

She said, "OK girl, alright, that'll be fine. Just call me in the morning. If I haven't already got me a ride by, then I'll get you to take me. I just really don't wanna bother Marissa."

I said, "OK, I'll take you in the morning and by the time I check out I'll head your way." When I called her that morning, Marissa had already taken her to the hospital and they said she had cancer. She ended up passing, I think, within three to six days.

19

Unbelievable Loss

When I met Rosalee's roommate, things went south because he had a problem with me. He was stealing from her, and I called him out on it. Rosalee and I were making our own money, so we had no reason to steal from each other. We made the same amount, and we spent our money however we wanted. She would use her shift's earnings for what she needed, and I'd do the same for myself. We never needed anything, and when it came time to go out to eat, we'd either take turns paying or sometimes just cover each other's tab. It was never an issue.

Whenever we came into Memphis, we liked going to Celtic Crossing in Cooper Young, and we'd hang out with Alan, the bartender there, who was running for governor at the time. We'd have drinks, pay our tabs, and sometimes cover other people's tabs, too. When we made money, it wasn't just for us— we'd share it with the people around us. We didn't hoard it; we spent it as quickly as we made it, whether it was on Christmas gifts or things for our kids. It was all about enjoying what we had at the moment.

I remember being on the road, making money, and not being

able to be there physically for Chase, but I was always sending packages to my mom's house: sometimes shirts, another time it would be pants, sometimes it would just be toys, but it'd be different things. I knew how I felt when my grandmother would send me money for Valentine's Day in the mail. It was so cool to get a piece of mail and be a kid and then to get cash, so I try to do the same thing for my son, except for send him things that I know that he needed, but also like too. I remember one year when I flew out. That's the year that Rosalee and her roommate got into it and she had left where he was. Well, she didn't come back to anywhere. This is the last month and so I was moving things out of there.

We went down to Mexico in November, we went down to Mexico to see her dad and her dad was trying to get us to bring shit back over the border then, and we were like no fucking way. We already know that we're going to get stopped because, A) I stick out like a sore thumb and B) our tags are from fucking Memphis. They're definitely gonna stop us. On the way there, you never hit any type of traffic; there are no problems. But, when you come back, you hit every X-ray machine. They have machines that go all around the car. We got pulled out a couple of times, but thank God we told her dad that we were not bringing shit over. He had security with us while we were there, and we stayed for about a week. People came to the house to do our nails, and we even had our fortunes read. What's crazy is when the fortune teller read mine, she predicted I would have a second son with someone from Chicago, and she described everything about him—his skin tone, eye color—down to the details. At the time, I didn't think much of it, thinking I never really take those things seriously, but something told me to record it, so I did, and I never got rid of it.

While I was in Mexico, about three days in, I got an unexpected call from Luke. We hadn't talked in a long time, so when he called, I was surprised. He told me that Lee, Jr., Lucy's brother, Honeycakes, had died. It made the front page of the news. When he told me, I didn't know what to do. I just hung up the phone and immediately called Lucy. She confirmed it and sent me the newspaper article. I couldn't believe what had happened.

Honeycakes' cousin borrowed their lawnmower, and Papa Lee needed it back to cut the grass. He was going to pay Honeycakes. to do it, so Jr. went over to get the lawnmower back. When he arrived and they exchanged words, Rich Jr. turned his back and started walking toward Papa Lee's house. That's when they shot him. Honeycakes. tried to defend himself, but his gun jammed. He fired it as much as he could, but eventually, he couldn't breathe anymore.

Mama May saw everything from the porch and ran to her son, but they shot her once while she was running toward him. After that, everyone scattered. Papa ran toward his wife and son. Lucy ran off the porch to get to her mom and brother as fast as she could. She told me they just couldn't save Honeycakes. He passed away. That hurt me so much. I felt so helpless. There was nothing I could do; I wasn't there, couldn't be there for my friend, couldn't save them. There was no one I could call, no way to fix it. Now, Lucy had lost her nephew, her brother, and her mom had been shot. Three days later, I was returning from Mexico, heading back into Memphis.

Lucy shared her memories from this tragic day in both of our lives: *Dad had some lawn mower equipment that went missing, and we eventually figured out where it was. At the time, I was dating someone named Harry, and together, we went to retrieve*

156

it. Once we had the equipment, my mom went around the corner to confront her cousin about his father stealing from my dad. The situation quickly escalated.

The cousin was at a neighbor's house down the street, and when my mom confronted him, he got defensive. Things spiraled when he pulled out a gun. My brother and my mom ended up in the middle of the street as he started shooting. My brother tried to return fire and ran between two houses at the end of the block to avoid being hit. My mom screamed, "I'm shot!" as she fell to the ground, and my brother kept trying to shield her.

Chaos erupted. He just kept shooting, and my brother was hit multiple times, falling to the ground in front of my mom. My dad came rushing out of the house; he had been in the bathroom when everything started, and ran toward my brother. My mom tried to roll my brother over, pulling him close, but it was clear he was fading. You could see it in his eyes—he was fighting to stay with us, but he was slipping away.

The ambulance took 48 minutes to arrive, far too long. My brother bled out from a gunshot wound to his arm and chest. He died in the street, surrounded by the family who loved him. It was devastating, and to make things even worse, it wasn't long after this tragedy that we found out my mom had cancer. It felt like the world was collapsing around us.

I couldn't let this slide. The guilty party was eventually arrested, but that wasn't enough for me. The pain he caused my family demanded justice—or at least, that's how I saw it in the world we lived in. Riverside wasn't like other places. It was a different kind of battleground, where people believed in an eye for an eye. He had taken someone I loved, and I felt it was only fair to take something he loved in return.

20

Shuga Mama

At this point, I was talking to my grandmother, and I told her, "I think I'm ready for a new dog. I've just taken so many losses, and it feels like I'm losing everybody one by one. I need someone who's going to be there for me, someone who won't leave. Yes, I have my son, but I don't get him the way I want to or the way I'm supposed to. I'm not the best mom or the best version of myself right now, and I know that's what's best for him."

She looked at me and said, "Baby, You're right. Let's go look for your dog. Come on, are you ready?"

I replied, "Yeah, but I don't have the money. I only have this much."

She said, "Don't worry, I'll have the rest." In my head, I was wondering how she could afford it, but Goggy was always so tricky. She had a way of making you think one thing, but always had a trick up her sleeve and Mom was always right there to back her up.

We went to look at dogs, and they brought out a Shih Tzu, a Golden doodle, and even a Husky. None of them felt right.

Goggy said, "No, she doesn't need anything big. She needs something small, something that can fit in her purse."

The lady said, "Well, we have this dog, but nobody really wants her. I'll bring her out if you want to see her."

Goggy, never one to back down, said, "Are I sure? Bring her out." The lady hesitated but then went to get the dog. Goggy looked at me and said, "Go on, Cry Baby, go over there and check her out."

I went inside the small rectangular play area where the dogs were, and there was already one Shih Tzu inside. They brought out another Shih Tzu and put it in with the first one, but when they placed the other dog—this Pekingese—into the pen, she wasn't trying to impress anyone. She just stayed in the corner, observing. The other Shih Tzus started playing, jumping around, and trying to show off.

But not this little Pekingese. She wasn't interested. When one of the Shih Tzus jumped in front of her, she growled. That's when the Pekingese ran straight up to my grandmother.

Goggy smiled and said, "Yep, this is the one we want. I want the one nobody else wants."

The lady tried to persuade us, saying, "I might want to reconsider. The Shih Tzu is cheaper. The Pekingese is purebred and rarer, so it's going to be more expensive."

Goggy was firm, "How much?"

The lady said, "Well, the Pekingese will be $1,980. But, ma'am, I'm not sure that's something you and your grand-daughter can afford."

Goggy didn't hesitate. "Oh, that's not a problem at all. But if I pay that, you're throwing in a kennel, leash, dog food, and bowls. I want the full package for this dog that I say nobody wants. She's going home with a family that wants her today."

The lady looked a little taken aback, but nodded. Goggy looked at me, and I looked back at her, and we both smiled. I felt so happy at that moment.

Goggy said, "Come on, baby, let's go get your dog. Pick out the leash, pick out the kennel—pick what I want. We're getting this dog."

"Okay," I said. "But Goggy, what should we name her?"

Goggy thought for a second and said, "I don't know. We'll figure that out later. Right now, let's just get the damn dog." Then she turned to the lady and added, "And I want the papers. I want to know her birthday and see her shot records."

So, after everything was settled, the lady—KiKi, the one who sold us the dog—gathered the paperwork and shot records.

My grandmother, being thorough as always, asked, "And if something goes wrong with this dog, then what? We just spent all this money and don't have a dog?"

KiKi reassured her, "No ma'am, we have a policy. It's right here. If anything goes wrong, just call us, and we'll make it right."

"Okay, thank you," my grandmother said. And with that, we were on our way home. On the car ride, we started thinking of names for her.

I said, "She's just so cute. She looks like a little fox."

Goggy agreed, "Yeah, You're right. But we've got to think of a name. How about Little Foxy?"

I laughed and said, "No."

She then said, "Well, what do I think? She kind of looks like brown sugar, doesn't she?"

I thought for a second and said, "Yeah, maybe we'll just call her Shuga."

So that was it. Goggy officially called her Shuga, and that

was her name on paper. But as time went on, Shuga's true personality began to show. She was so calm, never yapping or barking, and always so prissy, almost like a mom. She never bit or growled, just always so well-behaved. My grandmother had a way of picking the perfect dogs, and Shuga was no exception. I didn't know how she knew, but she always picked the best ones.

As Goggy spent more time with her, she started calling her "Shuga Mama," as she reminded her so much of a mom. I couldn't help but laugh because there was a character in one of my favorite cartoons, *The Proud Family*, named Shuga Mama, and she was the grandmother of the family. It just felt so right.

So one day, I said, "Goggy, why don't we just call her Shuga Mama?"

Goggy smiled and said, "Yeah, baby, I think that fits her better. She is a Shuga Mama." And that's how Shuga became Shuga Mama. From that day on, she was Shuga Mama, our little girl, and she never left our side.

When we first brought Shuga Mama home, everything seemed fine for the first two or three days. But soon, we noticed something wasn't right. Every time she needed to use the bathroom, she'd let out this high-pitched whine. It was heartbreaking, and I immediately knew this wasn't normal. I called my grandmother, Goggy, for advice. Goggy had experience breeding Shih Tzus back in the day to make extra money while working two jobs to support her kids and grand kids.

She was the first to say, "That's not right. You need to get her to a hospital."

I rushed Shuga Mama to the vet, and they confirmed she had a hernia that required immediate surgery. My heart sank when they told me the cost—another $2,000 on top of what we'd just spent to get her. We'd only had her for three days, and I couldn't believe this was happening.

I called the breeder, explaining the situation, and they suggested we exchange Shuga Mama for another dog or get a refund. Goggy wasn't having it.

She told them point-blank, "No, we're not doing that. You sold us this dog, and now you need to make this right. We're not letting her die because you don't want to pay for the surgery." Goggy even threatened to get lawyers involved, and she was so upset that she hung up on them.

About thirty minutes later, the breeder called back with a very different tone. He apologized for the situation and offered to cover all the medical expenses.

Goggy, always sharp, told him, "Now you're making sense. We've already spent money with you. You need to make sure we feel comfortable continuing to do business with you."

Thanks to Goggy's persistence, the breeder followed through and paid for everything—surgery, pain medication, and follow-up care. Shuga Mama pulled through beautifully, and we were so relieved. She's our girl, and from that moment on, she was part of the family. No one was going to take her away from us. That's how we got through Shuga Mama's hernia ordeal, and now she's thriving, loved, and spoiled as she deserves to be.

21

Pimp Phat Daddy Kane

I remember a time when Bobby said he was going out to hustle, but when he came home, he was covered in scratches and hickeys. His neck, arms, and back were marked up, and I could tell he'd been with someone. When he walked in, I came out of the kitchen and asked him where the hell he'd been.

He said, "I've been on husband and baby duty, like I told you."

I told him, "That's what you said, but that's not what your skin tells me. You look like a damn cheetah. Are you serious?"

He tried to play it off, saying, "No, babe, I wouldn't do that to you. I promise." But I knew better.

I said, "Yes, I would, because I've done it before." I was getting tired of his lies. So, we argued. He left for a few hours, then came back with a bunch of stuff— a watch, a Coach purse, and some Coach perfume. It was all matching, but I wasn't impressed. I told him, "I don't want this crap. Nine times out of ten, it's fake. I know you went to Smokey City and got it from a booster."

He tried to convince me it was real, but then admitted, "I

stole it from the mall."

At that point, I didn't even know what to do but laugh. At least he tried, but I knew it was over. He was doing the same thing that men before him had done, just like when Maine Maine had cheated on me. It was the same pattern, just less and less respect each time. I wasn't going to take it anymore. Terry never laid a hand on me, though. Chicago didn't either. Bobby tried once, and I beat his ass, and he never did it again. After that, I refused to take any kind of abuse.

When Smokey City was wrapping up, that's when Little Steve died—Bobby's friend. After that, Bobby had to find somewhere else to go. He was out on bond at the time. We stayed at his grandmother's house a couple of nights, washing our clothes and getting by. Eventually, though, things faded between us, and I went back to Lucy's. A month later, Bobby called me to say he was going to jail. He told me he'd be gone for a long time—20 or 30 years— and that was that. To this day, he's still in jail, and that was the end of Smokey City with him. But when Phat Daddy came into the picture, that was a whole other side of Smokey City I had never experienced. After that, I had to pack up and move. That's when I left Goggy's place and moved into an apartment across from Stephenson's. Now, things were getting interesting. I'd been through a lot, including the cartel stuff—going down to Mexico, making trips back and forth. And then Rosalee had her own trouble when she caught someone stealing and eventually ended up losing her place in Texas. When I moved into that apartment, that's when Phat Daddy Kane entered the picture.

Rosalee had mentioned that she was only talking to her mom occasionally, so I figured it was just me and her handling business. But that's when things started going wrong with the cartel. Shipments started missing stuff. Neither Rosalee nor I used dope, so it didn't make sense. Turns out, Rosalee wasn't telling me that we were dropping off the drugs at her mom's place, where her mom had her own operation. But Melissa, who was handling the drops, started dipping into the dope, using it herself, and then claiming she hadn't touched it. So, by the time the guys received the shipments, they were short. This caused major problems for the cartel. The drugs weren't arriving on time, and Melissa's actions were wrecking everything.

I didn't know it at first, but Melissa's addiction to getting high was ruining the whole operation. She was using the drugs for herself, and things weren't getting done right. It became clear that Melissa was messing everything up, and that's when the problems started escalating with the cartel. The situation got worse when I realized Melissa had a history of getting into trouble in Atlanta, and that's as far as we ever went. Had I known that from the beginning, I would've never been involved.

Around this time, things with my family started getting real tense. My parents knew something was up, but they didn't say anything. Then one night, my dad pulled me aside at a Mexican restaurant.

He said, "Whatever you're doing, stop."

I denied it, but he insisted he knew better. He told me I was getting too deep, and that was the turning point. Right after that conversation, the feds called me in, and I knew I had to step back. I did one more trip, then cut ties completely. I stopped answering the phone, and I focused on making money on my own.

At that point, I moved into an apartment off Summer and Macon. I was working with Hank, doing dates, and he had his own thing going. Rosalee was still doing her thing, but we eventually drifted apart, though I still cared about her and was there for her if she ever needed anything. Hank and I had a good system going, pulling off jobs and making money. He would introduce me to people he worked with, and I would work with them too, just in different ways. Hank used his connections for contacts and deals, while I was getting money through other means.

One night, Hank introduced me to a guy who helped with lower prices on certain things, which worked out well for both of us. The system was simple: we helped each other get what we needed. On slow nights, when I didn't have dates, Hank would help me out, and vice versa.

At the same time, Hank was pulling off car thefts. I wasn't into buying lavish things, but we'd hit cars if we needed to. Hank and his crew were smooth operators, always staying ahead and making plans for everything. I remember one night when I was late on my car payment and was trying to hide it from being towed. We parked it between two cars in a way that made it impossible to see, just to keep it a little longer before it was taken. It was a constant balancing act, just doing what we had to do to keep things moving, even if it meant doing things the hard way.

Hank and Clyde had already gotten out of the car and were walking up toward the apartment. I was still inside, grabbing my purse, phone, and making sure I had everything I needed in case they towed the car. I didn't want anything valuable left behind. Just as I was locking the car, a man came out of nowhere. He didn't say anything, but I saw the laser beam from a gun pointed right at me. It was a white guy, and he had a gun trained on me.

I immediately put my hands up and said, "Please don't shoot."

He responded, "I saw you, and I saw two black guys. Where are they?"

I replied, "They live with me. Those are my boys." I kept pleading, "Please don't shoot," for a third time, but he didn't seem convinced.

He scoffed, "Yeah, right. Two black guys are your boys?"

By now, I could feel the tension rising as I saw the beam on my chest. The guy was shaky, holding the gun unsteadily, but the laser stayed steady. Then, I looked behind me and saw Clyde and Hank's beams—Clyde's was red, and Hank's were green, pointing right at him.

I turned around and said, "That's them. Everybody put your guns down. We all live here."

The guy looked at me, still suspicious, and asked, "Where do you live, and why are you parking all the way down here?"

I explained, "My car's under repossession. I've been parking here the last couple nights to keep it from being towed."

He seemed to relax a little, realizing he'd seen the car there the night before but didn't know whose it was. He followed me up to my apartment, checked my key, and walked in with me to confirm that I lived there.

Once he saw everything checked out, he said, "Well, now that I know you live here, I feel a lot better. Man, I'm sorry about that. To be honest, I wasn't going to shoot you. I just had to make sure everything was okay. I'm a single dad, raising my kids alone after losing my wife."

I could understand. He said, "Can I give you something to calm down? Weed, pills, anything? I know you must be shaken after that."

I declined, saying, "No, it's fine. I'd just appreciate it if I'd let me park my car between yours and the neighbor's car." He agreed, and from that moment on, we were cool with each other.

I was still on Macon and Bobby was still calling, checking up on me every now and then. One day, I told him I couldn't find any weed and asked if he knew anyone. He gave me Little John's number, a guy in Smokey City, off Decatur. I bought from him a couple of times, but I could tell he wasn't about anything serious. He was one of those guys who was probably just using whatever money he had to fund his habit. I wasn't looking for that type of drama, so I kept my distance.

Then one day, when Little John wasn't around, I went next door to ask if anyone had any weed. That's when this big, heavyset guy with a gray beard and hair came out and said, "I got I covered. And if I don't have it, I'll make sure we get it."

I introduced myself, but I could never remember his name, so me and Lucy just called him "Phat Daddy Kane." We didn't know why we came up with that name, but it fit. He was a pimp, and we thought it was funny. Phat Daddy Kane and I got close, but we never had any personal involvement beyond business.

The whole situation was getting more intense and, honestly, more dangerous by the day. Phat Daddy Kane was deep into his hustle, selling crack. I never had an issue with him, but things were starting to get darker. At one point, Hank suggested I take over one of his trap houses, since Phat Daddy Kane's was running on fumes. Hank had the connections, and I had my own stash. The thing with Phat Daddy Kane was, he only sold crack—if I needed anything else, I had to go elsewhere.

His house, what we called a "shotgun house," had three rooms before you got to the back. It was pretty grimy, but it worked. Phat Daddy Kane had three locks on the door, and I was the only one with keys to all of them. People were not happy about that, especially the other guys running their own operations. Having a white girl with that much access to everything didn't sit well with them. But that's just how things were starting to go.

During my time hanging out with Phat Daddy Kane, I started to get a real sense of the streets. Phat Daddy Kane was connected, and he had his right-hand woman and a couple of other people working for him. His main woman didn't like me much, but she had to play it cool because that's what Phat Daddy had instructed her to do. In a way, it was similar to my own situation with Maine Maine—she had to deal with me, just like I had to deal with him. But I wasn't going anywhere, and I wasn't going to let anyone push me around.

I was becoming a leader in my own right. I didn't follow orders; I gave them. A simple look from me could get things done. If I wanted something, it was taken care of. If I looked at someone a certain way, I didn't need to speak—everyone knew what to do.

I made connections with people outside of his usual network. I told him I could get him things other than just crack, like weed and heroin, so he started working with me, especially with the weed, which was more common at the time. The heroin connections were riskier, but it was all part of the game.

I found myself sitting at meetings with all the big players—some of the most important people on the street. Phat Daddy Kane would bring me into these gatherings, where everyone would sit down at a table, sometimes with security at the door in case things went south. The first couple of meetings were a bit of a surprise to me, but after that, I was trusted. He introduced

169

me to everyone in the room, and word started to spread that I was someone to work with. He told them I could handle business, and if I needed something, they should take care of it and send him the bill.

Before long, I was connected across several parts of Memphis. Phat Daddy Kane's people in Castalia were aware of me, and so were the folks over in Hillview, North Memphis, and Decatur. I wasn't just a player; I was now stamped in multiple areas. I didn't need to attend every meeting after that because my reputation spoke for itself. My status in the streets was solid, but I wasn't on the block all the time—I had a child to think about and couldn't risk getting caught up.

Phat Daddy Kane would go off with his main woman, leaving me in charge at the trap house. I was handling everything— managing the work, keeping an eye on things, and making sure that everything ran smoothly. There were guns around for protection, including AK-47s, and I was always ready for anything that went down. But there was something strange about one of the things he had in the house: bombs. He kept these homemade bombs around, right next to the stove where the crack was cooked. It never made sense to me. The bombs were dangerous, and with everything moving so fast, I didn't question it at the time. I just kept my head down, played the role of the quiet outsider, and did what needed to be done.

There was one time when we had a "hood trial" because someone stole a $5 hit of crack from Phat Daddy Kane's room. Yes, a $5 hit of crack. The trap house was full of regulars— junkies who came in and out every day to buy and get high—but some of them thought they had a say in things, like deciding on punishments or playing judge. So, the trial went down. Everyone pointed to this one girl as the thief. They even put her in the same chair I used to watch everything go down. Turns out, that chair was the one used for interrogations. Phat Daddy Kane asked her where she was when he was in the back and the door was open. She was by his room, right by the door. And when he realized the crack was gone, she was nowhere to be found. She came back later, high as a kite. Everyone knew it was her.

He asked the room, "Who thinks she did it?" And everyone raised their hands. There was no doubt in anyone's mind. Then came the hard part—what was her punishment? People wanted her to be beaten, but I didn't want to see that.

I spoke up and said, "Babe, I know exactly what she can do to make it right."

I walked up to him and whispered in his ear, suggesting that she clean the bathroom and kitchen instead. I didn't want her to get hurt, so I tried to shift the focus off her. He agreed and told her that she would have to clean up. She looked at me, grateful, knowing I had helped her avoid a much worse fate. I made it seem like his decision, but I was pulling the strings behind the scenes.

That was one of the two hood trials I witnessed. The second time, things were getting more intense. People were coming in and out of Phat Daddy Kane's place, and I started to worry about getting caught.

I told him, "If the feds come in, I'm going down for all this because I'm the white girl here. Everyone else will walk away, but not me."

He agreed, and I told him we needed to get rid of the new people coming in—only the regulars should be allowed. We couldn't afford to draw attention.

I even felt like we were being watched. Hank, who was picking me up and dropping me off, noticed a car parked nearby, and we both started to get paranoid. So, I took it to Phat Daddy Kane, telling him things needed to change. He had to tighten up security and cut off access to the house for anyone who wasn't a regular. He started moving things around—guns, dope, whatever he could stash—getting rid of anything that might tie him to the house. He had people dig holes in different yards and bury weapons. It wasn't just the dope that needed to be hidden—it was everything that could get us caught.

He started taking more precautions, limiting access to the house. The trap house became a lot quieter after that, with fewer people hanging around. We were trying to clean up, and I wanted him to stay safe, but we knew it was only a matter of time before things went south. We couldn't tell who would get hit first—our house or someone else's. All we could do was brace ourselves and hope we weren't the ones to get caught.

So, Phat Daddy Kane started moving things around, adjusting the way he operated. I told him to stop cooking up all his dope at once because I've got people who want Coke too, and he wasn't about that life.

He'd say, "I don't mess with Coke heads. They'll steal from I. Crack heads? They just want to work and get high, but they won't rob you."

I didn't fully get it at the time, but now I understand exactly what he meant. Looking back, I'd rather deal with a crackhead every day of my life than a coke head for a single day. I can appreciate that, though. I didn't want any thieves around me either.

Things kept moving, and I kept doing my part—serving people. I was running a little operation out of his place, pulling up with all sorts of things: Coke, crack, weed—whatever someone needed, I had it. My people were pulling up regularly for their orders.

Now, this was around the time I was driving the Jeep he got me, and things between me and Hank got pretty heated. We didn't usually argue, but when we did, it was always one of those "shut the fuck up" kind of situations. We'd go back and forth, but it would blow over quickly. However, one argument stands out.

This time, I was drunk—had a half-bottle of Maker's Mark in me—and I told Hank, "You think I care about you? I don't even care about myself. I don't care about you, or Phat Daddy Kane, or this truck, or anything else. I'll walk away from all of this, just like I've done before. It means nothing to me."

I didn't even remember what we were arguing about, but I do remember how I felt. Hank told me to shut up and go inside. I think he figured I was just talking out of anger, because I never really had to prove myself to him. Hank always had my back, and he knew when it was time to ride, I would ride. But at that moment, I wasn't thinking straight. And we were both caught up in whatever we were arguing about.

We got into it so badly that I wrecked the Jeep on purpose. Hank thought I was just talking, saying things like, "You won't do this. You won't do that." I said, "I won't? Watch me." I was over it, so I decided to take control. I was driving straight, but then I jerked the wheel to the right, making a sharp U-turn— just like the time I wrecked a car when I was younger. I hit a light pole, and the pole came down, causing the electric wires to snap and swing loose, sparking and crackling everywhere like snakes in the air. It looked dangerous; fire could've easily started from the sparks.

Hank got out of the Jeep without a scratch, but I was stuck

inside. I tried to get out, banging on the door, but I was trapped. Hank saw I was stuck, and the situation was about to turn deadly. The broken wires were sparking, and it was only a matter of time before a fire started. Hank didn't hesitate. He busted open the Jeep and pulled me out, saving my life. As we walked away from the wreck, Hank said, "Man, I can't stand you."

I shot back, "I don't give a fuck, I don't like you either."

He snapped, "You need to like me, I just saved your ass."

And I told him, "I fucking hate you."

We walked down the street, not talking. We were on Macon and Graham, at a three-way stop sign, and I knew how to get back to the apartment, but Hank didn't. He didn't know the area, so he had to figure it out. I got back to the apartment two hours before him, but I still couldn't get in. I was busy trying to be smart, but in the end, I still needed him. He was still there for me, and that was something we'd never forget.

The next day, I had to tell Phat Daddy Kane that I'd totaled the Jeep. I told him someone hit me, and I had to walk away because I didn't have a license or registration. He knew I didn't have those things because he bought the car from a crackhead. He just took the loss and didn't make a big deal out of it. The very next day, he bought another car—a little red Honda Civic—and gave it to me. It wasn't mine officially, but we all knew I'd be driving it.

By then, Josh was still around, but he wasn't involved like he used to be. He got the hint that things were going downhill. He wasn't even giving me money anymore, and that's when I started hanging around Phat Daddy Kane more. When I was with him, I never left empty-handed—whether it was weed, gas money, cash, or even food. Phat Daddy Kane was good to me. He became like my sugar daddy in a way. I worked the game, but I did it differently—classier, gentler, and in a way that I think caught him off guard.

He said, "Man, you're just like me."

By this point, Phat Daddy Kane had already taught me everything there was to know about getting money in the game. He showed me how to break it down, cook it up, and if needed, cook it again. He taught me the right amounts of baking soda and water to use, how to mix it, and how to make the crack come back just right. At this point, I was the one bringing the sauce back to him, cooking it up, breaking it down—he only had to open his door and make sure it was all set because I knew exactly what to do.

They started saying for a while that the white girl in Smokey City had the best crack. I can't lie, they said if you wanted it, that's where you needed to go. It was like Rice Krispies when I heard it popping; I knew it was good. But the truth is, I never tried it, so I couldn't speak for it. How could someone so good at selling and cooking drugs never touch them? I guess it just shows that you can adapt to anything, learn any environment, and if your head's in the right place, you'll get out. You can't let it consume you, though—it's all about mind over matter. You have to know it's temporary, that you're going somewhere. If you're stuck, it's because you chose to be.

By this point, I had gotten really close with Phat Daddy Kane. His girl had gone to jail, and the other two women around him were basically there to get high, sell themselves, and bring him the money. I was the only one who didn't have to do that, which didn't go unnoticed.

One of the other girls finally spoke up and asked, "Why doesn't she have to do what we do?" Kane didn't even hesitate—he knocked her out cold with one punch. Her tooth flew out, and after that, she never spoke to him like that again. It was so casual, like it was nothing.

He looked at her, completely unfazed, and said, "Pick your tooth up off the ground and get out of my face."

Even as she apologized, calling him "Daddy" and begging for a hit of crack, he barely reacted. He only gave her a hit because she'd lost a tooth, saying, "Fix that shit." He handed her what I'm pretty sure was my $5 worth of crack and dismissed her.

At this time, Hank was still around, picking me up and dropping me off.

Kane noticed him and asked, "Who's he to you?"

I told him, "That's my nephew."

He gave me a look and said, "You're white; that's not your nephew. Who is he *really*?"

I explained, "He's my son's cousin, so I call him my nephew." Kane seemed to accept that.

Eventually, I got Kane cool with Hank. Hank didn't stay around much because there wasn't anything in it for him, and honestly, I didn't really need him there. I had the keys, the locks, the guns—I could handle myself.

Lucy, on the other hand, would sometimes pull up when I called her, but she never came inside. She knew what kind of place it was—a lion's den where anything could happen. But me? I walked in like I owned the place because, in a way, I did. Kane made it clear that when he wasn't around, I was the one in charge. I called the shots, made deals, and decided who got what.

I even got to the point where I was telling people what to do. If the place was messy, I'd say, "Clean this up, and I'll give you a $5 hit." And they did it because they knew I spoke for Kane.

On top of the drugs, Kane also sold snacks, drinks, and random stuff like Slim Jims and Hostess cakes.

Once a month, Kane would stock up at Sam's Club, buying snacks and drinks to sell alongside everything else. When people came to buy their crack or other drugs, they'd often grab a snack or drink while they were there. It made sense—they were already coming to him, so why bother going to a store? Kane made double what he paid for the items, turning it into another hustle on top of the drug business.

There were a few times when I hung out in the house and actually had fun. We'd sit in the front room and play Spades, and Kane couldn't believe how good I was. I was winning left and right, taking names, and making people leave their seats for the next round. Kane and I made a great team because we didn't lose.

He was so impressed that he said, "Let me throw something on the grill for us."

That night, he went to the store, bought lamb chops, and cooked them up. We ate together in his room because staying out in the open meant people would start hovering, asking for things or trying to get his attention. There was this one guy, kind of like a "runner," who did whatever was needed—warming up the car, running errands, grabbing a beer, or going to the liquor store. When Lucy came over, I'd already have weed ready and would tell him to grab a cigar. He'd bring it back right away.

Lucy and I would sit in the car laughing about it.

She'd say, "What the fuck? Why are these people listening to you?"

We'd crack up because neither of us could believe it. I mean, who was I? Just a girl fresh out of abusive relationships, barely scraping by. Even though I was at my lowest, I told myself I'd rather be at rock bottom selling dope than selling my body.

I had family members who did drugs, but I didn't sell to all of them. There were a couple of exceptions—my uncle and aunt asked me for heroin, so I sold it to them. They wanted to do it together, but I never touched it. I never used cocaine, heroin, or crack.

The only painkiller I ever tried was a Loritab after getting my wisdom teeth pulled, but it made me so sick I didn't want to take it again. I've taken a Percocet a couple of times when I was in serious pain—like when I broke a finger after we hit a lick—but even then, I'd split a 30 mg pill into four pieces. One piece for me, and the rest went to Big D, Curse, or whoever else needed it. It wasn't much—just enough to take the edge off. I only did that once or twice because I hated it. I've always avoided pills unless I absolutely needed them for pain.

Weed has always been my thing, ever since my cousin first introduced me to it. I've been smoking since then and never really stopped. It was different from other drugs, though.

My mom used to say, "Once you start a drug, you won't be able to stop." That warning stuck with me, and it's probably why I never wanted to touch anything harder.

Lucy would come around and hang out, but she never wanted to go inside the house. She said the vibe just wasn't for her. But there was this one time Kane left for a few days to stay at a hotel.

Before he left, he called to check in, saying, "I'll be gone for three days. You good?"

I told him I was fine and asked, "Do you mind if I have a friend come over?"

He hesitated and asked, "What kind of friend?"

I replied, "A girl. She's just coming to chill for a little bit."

He said, "That's fine, but she can't stay too long."

"Don't worry," I reassured him. "She's nervous about even coming inside. I just want her to see where I'm at in case anything happens to me. She's the only person I can really call family right now."

He agreed, but I still stuck to the rules. I didn't want to risk anyone telling him she stayed longer than she should or that I broke his trust. Back then, I followed instructions to the letter—it was how I survived.

Lucy finally came over that day, and it was funny because I'd been up all night selling crack for the past two nights. I made some good money, and when she came, I wanted her to feel safe. Kane wasn't due back until that evening, so I had the place to myself.

"Come with me," I said. "It's just me back there, and I've got the keys. I can lock the door, and nothing will happen."

She looked uneasy. "Girl, I don't know about this."

"Trust me. I've got you. You know I've got you."

Reluctantly, she got out of the car, and we walked up to the stoop. The do-boy was hanging around, so I gave him a heads-up. "Hey, I've got company in the back. I'm not selling anything right now, and I don't want to be bothered."

He nodded. "Alright, I'll keep people away as much as I can. But if one or two slip through and knock, just don't answer."

"I got you," I said. "Thanks."

Lucy followed me inside, still cautious, but once we were back there, it was chill. I locked the door, and for a little while, it felt like a regular hangout—just two friends smoking and laughing.

Lucy and I walked into the first room, and she immediately

179

looked around, wide-eyed. "This is crazy," she whispered. "You have to let people know what you know."

I laughed lightly and said, "Just stick with me; it's going to get wilder. Follow me."

The first room was chaos. People were sprawled out on the floor, high, some smoking crack, others shooting up. It was a haze of funk and desperation. Lucy looked uncomfortable, but I guided her through to the second room.

This room was different. There was a card table, a radio, and a mix of people drinking, smoking cigarettes, or rolling their weed. It was the middle ground—away from the crack smoke but still full of its own kind of energy.

Finally, we reached his room. There were three locks on the door, and I told Lucy, "Watch my back while I unlock these. I don't want someone coming at me from behind."

She nodded. "I got you. Just hurry up."

We kept our voices low, communicating silently with glances and quick nods. I unlocked the locks one by one, and we stepped inside. The sight hit Lucy like a wave.

There was a gun on the left-hand side, two more on the bed, and money spread everywhere. On the bed was a dinner plate set up like a clock, but instead of numbers, it was crack. Each "hour" was a $5 hit, carefully lined up like clockwork.

Lucy stared at it all and said, "Girl, what the fuck are you doing selling crack?"

I shrugged. "Hell," I said, "I'll sell anything at this point. I'm trying to get some money, trying to make something happen."

She shook her head. "I feel you, but this ain't the way, Cry Baby. This shit is not gonna end well."

"I know," I said softly. By then, we had already started smoking a blunt, the tension between us easing slightly.

A knock came at the door. "Who is it?" I called out.

"It's me," came the voice of a familiar junkie.

I cracked the door open. She wanted a $5 hit but only had $4. "No," I said firmly. "You need to come back when you've got the full $5."

I shut the door and another knock followed. This time it was someone who had the $5, though it was all in loose change. I made her count it out in dollars and hand it to me piece by piece. Once I had it, I tossed it onto the bed, handed her the hit, and closed the door again.

Lucy just watched the whole process, shaking her head. "Man, this shit is crazy," she said. "I hate you're going through this."

"Me too," I replied. "But right now, I've got to do what I've got to do. He said he'd give me a couple of guns, and I'm trying to get some protection since they stole my last one. I don't want anything in my name, though. If something goes down, I don't need it traced back to me."

"I get that," she said, still looking concerned.

We kept talking, and I told her about the stash of change he had. It was in one of those small bathroom-sized garbage cans, oval-shaped, about knee-high, and filled to the brim. I dumped as much of it into her purse as I could.

Lucy took it to a Coinstar machine later and ended up with enough cash to get by for a bit. That was how we were—always looking out for each other, sharing what we could, and keeping it real.

Even though Lucy left that day, I'll never forget how she always gave me a sisterly vibe. She didn't have much, and neither did I, but we had each other's backs in ways that mattered.

One time, there was a commotion happening in the front room. Meanwhile, Phat Daddy and I were in the back, each doing our thing. He was stacking his dope, organizing his money, and keeping everything meticulously separated. I was smoking my weed, texting, listening to music, and counting cash, putting it where it needed to go.

Phat Daddy had a system for everything—a pile for what he made off the dope, another for snacks, and yet another for cigarettes. He kept it all separate to track his profits and figure out if re-upping on something was worth it or if he should just let it go.

While I was deep in my zone, we heard the noise up front. Apparently, Little John had just bought some tabs, but then he turned around and stole some before buying bars. In the middle of that deal, a junkie tried to snatch the bars, and everything erupted.

The banging on Phat Daddy's door started. Over and over, the loud knocks were relentless. He finally snapped and yelled, "Hold the fuck up! Stop banging on my fucking door! Back the fuck up! Back the fuck up!"

And then he grabbed his gun.

He shot one round straight up into the air. Then, for reasons only he understood, he shot through our roof. My first thought was, *If he shot it straight up, isn't it coming right back down?* And why would he shoot through the roof and risk putting a hole in it?

But when I glanced up, I realized something that froze me for a moment. There were already several bullet holes in the ceiling. That's when it hit me—this wasn't his first time doing this. He'd done it before, and to him, it was just another day.

The chaos outside didn't stop, though. So Phat Daddy opened

182

the door, gun still in hand.

There were two female junkies fighting—fists flying, hair-pulling, the works. Nearby, two men were locked in a full-on brawl, neck and neck, pushing and grappling.

Phat Daddy started barking orders. "Get them and break them up! Hey, you! Stop this shit!"

But no one was listening. It was too far gone.

So, he fired again. "Hold the fuck up! This is my shit!"

The gunshot was enough to freeze everyone in place. The fights stopped, and silence fell across the room.

I was still standing by the door to our room, peeking out cautiously. Then Phat Daddy turned to me and said, "C, baby, get up here. Sit down in this black chair. You're gonna witness this shit."

I didn't argue. "Okay," I said and walked over.

"Do you want me to lock the door?" I asked, half-turning back.

He snapped, "I didn't tell you to lock the door. I told you to sit down."

"Okay," I repeated, and I did as I was told.

So, I sat down in the black chair like Phat Daddy told me. One of the junkies next to me was shaking so bad from fear that she couldn't even light her cigarette. She had just pulled it fresh out of the pack, and her hands were trembling so hard that the lighter slipped.

I gestured for the cigarette with my hand, mimicking the motion of smoking and tapping fake ashes, and she handed it to me to light. Once I lit it, I took a couple of hits myself. I was nervous—so nervous I could barely keep my composure. I didn't know what was about to happen, and from the look on her face, neither did she.

The two girls who had been fighting earlier were now huddled together in the corner. They went from clawing at each other to holding onto each other like their lives depended on it. It was surreal to watch them, both frozen in fear, clinging to one another. If they didn't know what was coming, and they'd been there way longer than me, then I was completely in the dark.

Phat Daddy shot up into the air again, commanding everyone's attention. I sat still in the chair, watching as the room's chaotic energy hung heavy in the air. The two girls stayed pressed into the corner, while the two guys stood tensely nearby. Little John had already left—he was expecting Phat Daddy to handle the situation and get his dope back. This was his house, and Little John was leaving it up to him to make things right.

Phat Daddy stood there, holding his pistol, and barked out, "Who's got the dope? Matter of fact, fuck that. Why the fuck are you two bitches arguing?"

He pointed the gun at both girls, the barrel sweeping between them. It was cocked and ready, and the way he moved it made it clear that one wrong word could send things spiraling.

The first girl stammered, "I bought some crack from you, Daddy, and she took half of my crack."

The other girl jumped in, yelling, "But I sucked his dick to get the money! I did what you told me to do, Daddy. I brought the shit back to you. But she said you had to get high first before I could smoke the rest!"

The back-and-forth went on for a moment before Phat Daddy's patience snapped. Without hesitation, he swung the back of the pistol at the first girl's head, hitting her hard enough to send her stumbling. "Shut the fuck up!" he shouted.

Then he turned his attention back to her, his tone deadly

184

serious. "Bitch," he said, "you out here sucking dick to bring money back for crack? You don't work for her anymore. You work for me now. Do you understand?"

She nodded frantically, tears streaming down her face. "Yes, Sir. Yes, Sir."

"Good," he replied, cold as ice. "Now take your ass outside, and drag your little friend's ass with you. Both of y'all are gonna work the streets all night. And you better bring me back some motherfucking money. You hear me?"

"Can I—can I just get some crack first?" she begged, her voice trembling. "I just need to get high before I go."

Phat Daddy sneered at her. "Bitch," he said, "I'm not giving you a fucking thing. And I don't even know if I'll give you shit when you bring me the money back."

"Yes, Sir. Yes, Sir," she whispered, broken and obedient.

And with that, the two of them scurried out of the room like roaches scattering when the lights come on.

Phat Daddy's voice cut through the room. "This ain't even the type of drugs I fucking sell," he growled. "I'm already letting you do this shit in here. Y'all aren't supposed to do anything but crack, weed, and cigarettes in this motherfucker.. You can drink if you want to—that's it. But all that other shit? That shit has to go. This is a fucking crack house, not a fucking trap house."

The tension in the room was suffocating, but the arguing started up again between the two men. As they were going at it, something fell out of one guy's pocket—pills. Phat Daddy's eyes locked onto them instantly.

"I told you he had them the whole time!" the other guy shouted, pointing. "But he was trying to put that shit on me!"

Phat Daddy's gaze shifted to the man with the pills. "Alright,

Johnny, you go ahead and get the fuck out of here," he said, gesturing toward the door. Johnny didn't hesitate; he left without looking back.

The remaining guy was already stammering. "Man, look, look, I was just trying to—look, I was gonna sell those and come to you! I was gonna get some money and come back for some crack. You—you know I don't do pills, man. You know that's not me. You know I get crack from you all the time!"

Phat Daddy stared him down, unflinching. "That's not my problem," he said coldly. Then he called over the Do Boy, one of his guys who handled his dirty work.

"Hold him down," Phat Daddy ordered.

The Do Boy grabbed the man, forcing him into a chair, his arms pinned in place. Phat Daddy walked over slowly, calm and deliberate. He pulled out a knife, its blade gleaming under the dim light.

"Hold his hand," Phat Daddy said.

The room felt frozen in time as the Do Boy pinned the man's hand flat on the armrest. Without a word, Phat Daddy brought the knife down, severing one of the man's fingers. Blood splattered across the floor, and the man's scream pierced the air, echoing through the house.

Phat Daddy turned to me, his eyes locking onto mine. "You see that?" he said, his voice low and menacing. "If you ever steal from me, or you ever pull some shit like he did, the same shit will happen to you. Maybe worse. You hear me?"

My stomach turned, but I nodded. "I understand," I said, my voice shaking but steady enough.

He leaned in closer, a twisted smirk on his face. "Good," he said. "Because I'm starting to like your fucking ass,. But if you ever feel like you have to lie to me, that's when we got a problem, and we'll need to fix it. You get me?"

"Yes, I understand," I replied. "But honestly, I think I'm gonna throw up."

He laughed, a cold, humorless sound. "Go ahead. Go back to the room. I needed you to see that—I needed you to know I don't play."

I didn't argue. I got up and walked back to the room, my legs feeling like jelly. My mind was racing, but one thing was crystal clear: this was what Phat Daddy called a "hood trial."

From that day on, "hood trial" became a permanent part of the vocabulary in Phat Daddy's world. Anytime something went down—if someone stole, lied, or crossed him—he'd ask with that same cold tone, "Do y'all want to go to hood trial? Do we need a hood trial in this motherfucker?"

Everyone knew what it meant. A hood trial wasn't some joke or a slap on the wrist. It was a full-on, twisted courtroom setup where you'd be judged, and the stakes couldn't be higher. If you were found guilty, there was no telling what you'd lose— a finger, a hand, or even your life. That night had been my first and only time witnessing it, and I realized later it was more than just about punishing the guy who stole. It was Phat Daddy making a point, teaching me a lesson I wouldn't forget. There weren't any other people in the room that time, and I'm convinced it was deliberate. He wanted me to see it up close, to understand the seriousness of crossing him.

That second hood trial? It was terrifying. I couldn't shake the image of the guy's severed finger or the sound of his scream echoing in my head for days. It was a warning, and I took it to heart. Phat Daddy didn't play, and if he said "hood trial," you knew it wasn't just a threat—it was a promise.

22

Payback

Looking back, I can't forget the time we were living in the Kirby apartment. That's the apartment where we got robbed, me and my son. It's tied to so many memories, but one of the most significant is the day Terry died, and it was right after my birthday.

I was born on May 9th; Terry's birthday was May 11th, so we'd been celebrating, having a good time for a couple of days. On the night of May 9th, we stayed up together—had fun, just being in each other's company. We watched movies, ate, and enjoyed the night. The next morning, on May 10th, I dropped Terry off at Lucy's house, at his granddad Papa Lee and May's place. Lucy, his aunt, was there too.

I told him, "Happy birthday, baby, I'll be back later with something for you," and he was cool with it. On May 11th, Terry came from his house in Whitehaven that he shared with India, mother of his child now. Justin, an old baseball teammate and classmate, dropped him off at Papa Lee's house. He walked two doors down to a neighbor's house while Lucy watched through the glass door.

In the meantime, I was at the apartment on Kirby in 2015, and I had a key to the place. I was on the phone with a Realtor, looking for somewhere else to move. I was planning to leave the apartment because of all the harassment and everything going on there. The Realtor wanted to meet me at a house on Colonial, and I told her I'd be there in 30 minutes. I was just walking into my apartment to change and head out when I got a call from Lucy.

She told me, "They killed my nephew." My heart sank, and I couldn't process it right away. Then she said, "Terry's gone! he's dead!" He had died in her arms.

Terry was born on May 11th, and he died on May 11th. It was no coincidence—it was a setup. They set him up, and he ended up being shot to death. I'll never forget that moment, how the day of celebration turned into a nightmare. It was one of the hardest days of my life, and it's something I carry with me every day. Once again, I walked into Hillview, but this time, the main trap was mine. I walked into Polo Lulu's trap, and soon, I was running the show there, too. I remember Tony's place off Hollywood. I walked into his trap and started making moves. It was fun now, but this time, I had a different plan. I wasn't just going to run it; I was going to take him for a ride. I'd get him to do the dirty work for me, while I stayed in the background, making my cuts without getting my hands too dirty. I needed something more, and I knew he could give it to me, so I was going to take advantage.

By this point, Hank, Big D, and I were still cool. They'd drop me off at spots, pick me up, whatever I needed. But then, my car got repossessed, and I didn't have a ride for a while. Not having a car made it hard to come over and see him, and he wasn't happy about it. He couldn't stand the thought of me being out of the loop for even a week.

So, what does he do? He buys a Jeep from a crackhead off Decatur Street. The thing wasn't much to look at, but it ran fine, and that was all that mattered. It was good enough to get me where I needed to go, and that's exactly what it did.

At this point, Lucy and I were still tight. We were still talking, but it wasn't just that. Lucy was like a sister to me, and I don't think she fully understood that, or maybe she didn't want to. She always called me her best friend, and I got that, but for me, it was deeper—we were sisters. The family she had built for herself became my family too. Blood doesn't always make you family; sometimes, it's the people who choose to stick by you.

As things unfolded, Lucy had finally decided to cut ties with Doodle. She gave him the option to go back home and think about their situation. They were on a break, but the girls kept calling her, calling her names, doing stupid stuff to bully her. It made no sense—it was all over a man she didn't even want. He was just around, and she still let him go, telling him he could have her if he wanted, but deep down, she didn't care about him anymore.

Meanwhile, they kept calling her, trying to stir trouble, but Lucy was done with him. I had just bought my son a paintball gun, something fun for us to do together. I needed to get it working, so when he came over, I figured it would be a good time to teach him how to use it. I went to Lucy's house, and we were trying to figure out if it worked, so we needed some target practice.

They were sitting on the porch, and I thought, why not use them as our targets? Just to have some fun. So, me and Lucy drove by and shot a few paintballs at the house—just to mess with them. We didn't hit anyone, but we wanted to intimidate them like they'd been doing to her for months: harassing her, hanging up on her, making posts on social media. It was relentless, and we were tired of it.

When they started laughing about the paintballs, I just shook my head. They should've been grateful it was paint and not a bullet. We didn't say much after that. We just left it alone, knowing we'd sent the message.

Whenever I made up my mind about something, when it was final, that was it. My mind was made-up, too. It was over. After I'd decided, I'd always text Lucy with an emoji. She knew exactly what it meant without me saying a word. Our little emoji code was our secret language, and it worked perfectly.

For instance, one emoji meant "wake up and check the news" because that was a sign that someone we didn't like had fallen or something had been taken care of. Another one meant "check the word on the street"—basically, I needed to make sure my name wasn't tied up in some mess. If I sent her another emoji, it was a way of saying, "Hey, check on this and see if I can come back home." One emoji meant, "Come get me," and if I sent her the emergency emoji, she knew something serious had gone down. We had it all mapped out. Our system was flawless.

One day, I sent her the emoji that meant "check the news." She woke up and saw it, and immediately texted back, "Oh my God." I just replied, "Nope, not over the phone. I'll be there in a second."

We never talked over the phone much because we knew the risk. Phones, especially those conversations, had a way of sticking around and causing problems. So, I went over to her house to tell her what had happened. When I got there, she couldn't believe it. "I can't believe you shot up that girl's

191

house," she said. I just shrugged. I had people at the front door, back door, and every window in that house. That house was hit."

She asked what happened and why I didn't tell her. But Lucy didn't know I was planning it. If she had known, she would've tried to talk me out of it.

She would've said something like, "No, don't do it. There are kids in the house" or something along those lines. But the truth was, they didn't care about that, so why should we? Lucy knew when I sent the emoji, she needed to check the news. But this time, when I pulled up to her house, she was in shock. "What happened? Who did this?" she asked.

I looked at her and said, "All you need to know is I was out there. I had five others with me. We went to the house, and when they started shooting at the front, we hit the back. They couldn't do anything but lay down and get down. That's the only way it was going to go down." She was stunned. "What the hell, friend?"

But she understood. All because I had to do it for her. She was my sister, no matter what. She wasn't my blood, but she might as well have been. She was the family I had left after losing Terry. At that point, it was just me and Lucy—our parents still around, but for how long? We didn't know.

Around that time, I was still hanging out with Phat Daddy Kane off Decatur St., running around Memphis, getting involved in all kinds of stuff. It wasn't just about the streets anymore; it was personal.

One night, I ran into the cousin, the one who shot Lucy's brother. I didn't kill him, but I made sure he felt it. I shot him and his partner, but I didn't finish the job. One of them went down with a leg wound, and I think the other did, too. The thing was, I wasn't trying to kill them, but I needed them to feel the pain that we were all living with. We lost a brother, and we almost lost our mom. They had to feel the same.

When I was with Tony, he was driving, and Hank and Claude were in the back seat. I asked them if they were sure. Tony looked at me and said, "Are I sure I wanna do this?" I told him, "If I don't, I will." And we made the U-turn. When I jumped out of that car, I wasn't thinking about anything but getting justice for my family. I shot him. They didn't die, but they felt it. I didn't stick around. I didn't have time to. There were cameras on the street. I didn't want them tracking the car back to us, so I made sure I was out before anything could get traced back.

That night, I sent Lucy the emoji again. She checked the news. When I pulled up to her house, we talked about it. We never talked about it again after that. We both knew the rules. We both understood. What happened was done, but I wasn't done. I was out there doing what had to be done for her. She'd lost her family, and I was the one who stepped up for her. She had my back, and I had hers. We were family. Always.

23

Busted By the Feds

By this time, we were settled in with the red car, and Phat Daddy Kane sent me out to grab breakfast the next morning. But on my way, I got a call.

The voice on the other end said, "Don't come back." I asked what was going on, and he said, "They hit the trap house. It's bad. There are cops everywhere. I'm not even there, so I don't know what they got, but it's not looking good. Did you leave anything at the house?"

I told him "No, I don't bring anything to leave behind."

He said, "Good, good. They won't have anything on you. They'll only have word of mouth, nothing they can really go off of."

I told him, "Alright," and we hung up. He called me back later that evening, around 5:00. He told me the house had finally cleared. They'd taped off the house next door, calling it a public nuisance. Our house wasn't marked that way yet, but he said it would be soon.

That was the first time they hit. Apparently, they didn't find much at our house, but they cleaned out everything next door. I think that's because when they hit us, everyone just spread out to the neighbors. It was a row of three trap houses, so when one got hit, everyone just moved to the next one. When they hit our house first, they didn't find anything because everyone had already moved everything next door. But when we got back, everything was torn up. I could tell they'd flipped everything over, destroyed it. When the feds hit, it's not about finding stuff— they just wreck everything because they can. It's not like they don't know how to search properly, they just come in, break everything up, and mess with you because they think you'll just go back and do it again. And when you do, that's when they catch you. It's a whole game, a scam.

So, we cleaned up the mess, got everything back in order, and got our junkies back in line. Nobody was scared to come by anymore. The block was rolling again. We had the grill going, junkies hanging out, doing their thing. We were probably making $10,000 a day, but even that wasn't much. By the time you re-up, pay the bills, buy groceries—you're just hustling to get by, just to make it another month. It was a never-ending cycle, and I was starting to see it wasn't going anywhere.

I was still hanging out, dating, doing my thing, but things with Josh were about to explode. And when I say explode, I mean everything was coming to a head. He stopped paying the bills, and now he wanted to take the apartment out of his name. Our situation had run its course. And honestly, can I blame him? If I'd been with someone for that long and done so much for them, only to get nothing back—hell, I'd be fed up, too. But at this point, it didn't matter. The lack of affection, the lack of anything real—it wasn't going to fix anything. I just had to let that go and take it as a loss. I sucked it up. And then, not long after, they hit the house again.

I was in the house talking to Phat Daddy Kane, and we were in the back room. By then, I'd gotten used to carrying this book bag. Instead of a purse, I carried a book bag because everything I needed was in there. A purse was too risky—I could leave it behind, and if I did, I'd be screwed. My book bag had everything I needed to get from one place to the next, always well thought out. I never did anything without thinking it through first. Sure, there were times I dove into situations without a plan, but I always managed to think my way out of them.

This time, though, I was on a roll. I wasn't carrying a purse anymore; I was carrying a book bag. In that bag, I always had a few packs of cigars, a pack of cigarettes, a beer or two, sometimes a bottle of Maker's Mark—whatever I might need for the day. I kept a phone charger and my phone in there, and a bottle of water in case I got too drunk. I stuck to the basics, just the essentials. And if I was re-upping or getting dope for someone, that's where I kept it too, because without a purse, it had to go in the bag.

The second time the feds hit, we were in the back room, and I had my book bag. The weird part is, he asked me the same day.

He said, "Why do I carry that book bag around? What happened to all those purses?"

I joked, "I haven't bought myself a new one, so I don't have anything to wear. Everything I have, I've gotten on my own."

He laughed and said, "So, this means I need to buy purses and shoes now? We have to upgrade?"

I said, "Right, we need to upgrade. I'm still stuck on the first page of the book when I should be at least halfway through."

He nodded and said, "I got you, we'll get you some soon. Just let me get back on my feet after this first hit. It hit me hard."

I told him, "Honestly, I've been keeping this book bag around because if the second hit happens, I'm running out that back door. And I swear to God, you don't know me, and I don't know you."

He replied, "I was gonna say the same thing. If anything happens, we don't know each other."

I said, "Alright, as long as we're on the same page."

Just as we were talking, we heard it—boom, boom, boom. People started scattering.

"So and so's address," someone shouted. "We have a warrant. We have permission to search more."

They gave us a few minutes to come to the door, show the warrant, and let them in. But I knew better than to answer that door. I had five minutes, tops, to get everything out. Flush everything if I could, stash what I can't. That was the rule of thumb.

While he was flushing, flushing, flushing, I was stashing. I grabbed all the weed I could find, all the money I could find. Hank was stuck at the house with no car, and I had gotten a ride there. I stuffed my book bag with everything I could carry—cash, weed, anything I'd be willing to take a charge for. I even grabbed three of his guns. I didn't have time to explain why, but I knew I needed protection, especially with what was about to go down.

I filled the bag and made my way out the back. He was in the bathroom, still flushing, and when he saw me, he shook his head and looked down. I didn't stop; I just shook mine and kept moving. I had to go. I had a kid. I couldn't do this anymore.

I recently drove by there, and Habitat for Humanity had tried to fix it up. They're trying, but it's just not the same. Back then, I went out the back door, and the feds hadn't made it back there yet. They were still on the side of the building. I had to be as quiet as I could. I couldn't climb over the fence because it would make too much noise, so I rolled under it. After that, I jumped over a wooden fence into someone else's backyard. I walked through their front gate and made my way down a whole new street.

I called Lucy and told her, "The feds just hit Phat Daddy Kane's house. Come and get me."

She dropped everything, met me at the liquor store off Jackson, right when I got off the exit. You go left, and right before you hit Decatur, there's a liquor store and a hotel called the Rainbow Inn. She picked me up from there, and I had to stay on the move, but I had to keep an eye out for her, too. There were feds everywhere.

I watched the liquor store from the motel, and when I saw her turn her car around, I walked over and jumped straight in. She took me straight to my apartment. When we got there, I told her everything that happened. She was in shock. I pulled out guns, weed, everything I had stashed, and she was telling me to put it all down.

She said, "I'll drop YOU off, but I'm going straight to Daddy's house."

I said, "Okay." After she dropped me off, I told her, "Call me when you make it."

I went inside, and Hank asked, "What happened? Did you rob him?"

I said, "Shut up. I didn't rob him. The feds hit the house, so I took what I could and ran. They got him, but they didn't get me." I told him I was waiting by the phone for Phat Daddy Kane to call, letting him know I had the goods but not the full extent of what I had.

Hank said, "Okay, I got you." And sure enough, Phat Daddy Kane called. I posted his bond with some fake paycheck stubs I made, and he was cool with it. He even let me keep the rest of the money and the three guns I took. He took the serial numbers off the guns so nothing could trace back to us. But little did I know, that was its own charge that would come back to bite me later.

Phat Daddy Kane was in and out of jail, going back and forth to court. Eventually, they took him in for good. The trap house was shut down, labeled a public nuisance. It hasn't been opened since. But it wasn't long before everything just moved two streets over. The people were still there, same faces, even some of the same crackheads, which was surprising.

It was at his point I realized something had to change. I couldn't keep on the path I had been on. With Phat Daddy in prison, and with the record I had already had, it was time to rethink my priorities. I couldn't keep putting myself in these situations; it was time to put myself and my child first. If only I had known what was coming for me next...

Photo Gallery

Amanda, Chase, and Hank

Pebble Beach

Goggy and Amanda

Granny Edra

Amanda and Chase

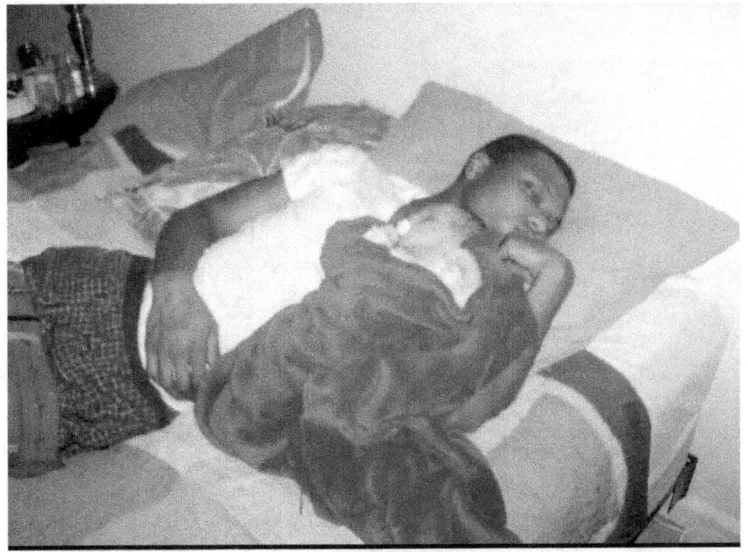

Cedric and Chase

Maine Maine and Cry Baby

Tony

Terry

Mama May and Cry Baby

Papa Lee and Cry Baby

Shuga Mama

Cry Baby
214

Bubble Bath

Benjamins

Bangers

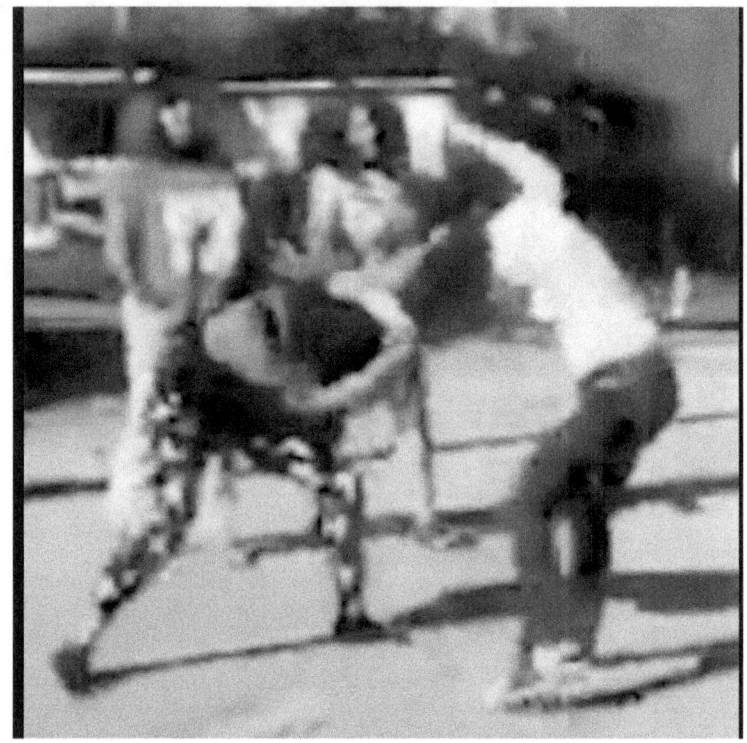

Girl Fight

Chosen Family Home

Hillview

Escape Window
221

Macon Road

Shootout over a Lawnmower Occurred Here

Cry Baby and Pimp Phat Daddy Kane

Cash

More of the Stash

Protection!

Hot Tub!

Payback!

Corner Store

Shhh!